MURDER IN A COUNTRY TOWN
and other stories

By Eric Lee

Paragon Publishing
Professional Fiction Publisher
El Sobrante, California, USA

Author website: www.ericleestories.com

For information address:

Paragon Publishing
Professional Fiction Publisher
2300 Greenridge Drive
El Sobrante, California, 94803

Author website: www.ericleestories.com

Substantial discounts on bulk quantities of this author's publications are available to corporations, educational disciplines, professional associations, and other qualified organizations. For details and specific discount information, visit ericleestories.com and click on the "Contact Us" link at the bottom of the website. For more information about the author's stories, visit ericleestories.com

Printed in the United States of America

Murder in a Country Town and other stories
    Eric Lee
    Library of Congress Catalog-In-Publication Data
    ISBN: 0-9674476-1-5

Table of Contents

Dedication

For all of my family and friends
who have supported my writing

Special thanks to the following people who have helped me greatly in my writing:

Alexandria Chun
John Cmelak
Ellen Hanscom
Gary Kurtzman
Brian Lee
Clarence Lee
Gloria Lee
Damon Maxey
Jaelynn Mayes
Bill Raynolds
Mike Sutton
Patrick Sutton
Michael Wiley

When My World Got Turned Upside-Down

"I'm sorry, but we have to work late tonight," my boss Tom told me at five o'clock, nearly three hours ago. I looked across the conference room table at him, and wondered if he sensed my irritation.

Piles of files and paperwork were scattered around the large table. For the last six and a half hours, we had been reviewing a proposed purchase agreement for our largest tax client. Trust me, it was a lousy way to spend a Friday night.

Around 5:30 that night, I had to call my fiancée, Kirstin, to cancel our plans for the night. At that point, I knew I wasn't getting home any time soon. I expected her to be upset because she had planned a nice, quiet evening at my place. Well, she was even more upset than I had expected. I didn't want to cancel, but as Tom had made it very clear, this *had* to be done tonight, so that our client could make a decision by tomorrow morning or the deal would be blown.

My legs were stiff and my back was a little sore from sitting down, hunched over paperwork. I got up to stretch, realizing that I hadn't gotten up from the chair in the last hour. I rubbed my sore eyes which felt the strain from many hours of reading fine print.

Noticing my movement, Tom took off his reading glasses and looked up at me. He was about ten years older than I, but the many wrinkles and gray hair that the business world had given him made him seem even older. He had been a good mentor to me. A partner at the firm, Tom had always looked out for me when promotions and raises were determined. "Mark, how you holding up?"

"I'm fine. My relationship with my fiancée, on the other hand, not too good."

"Didn't take tonight's cancellation too well, eh?"

I shook my head. "She's probably complaining to her roommate about me right now." I paused. "Tonight, we were going to celebrate the second anniversary of when you introduced us."

Tom showed a pained expression on his face. "Ouch. I wish you had told me."

"Would it have made a difference?" I asked, knowing the answer.

"No," Tom admitted.

I stared at him for a moment. "I have you to thank for getting Kirstin and me together, but if you keep me here late many more Friday nights, you're going to break us up."

"Look, I'll let you in on a secret that's kept my marriage alive." Since Kirstin was the daughter of one of our wealthiest tax clients, Tom always maintained a special interest in my relationship with her. "You're getting together tomorrow night, right?" I answered his question with a nod. "Write her a handwritten love letter and bring it with you tomorrow night. Mention your love and how much you're looking forward to being together as husband and wife." Tom sat back in his chair with his arms folded and a wide grin on his face. "Be sure to lay it on real thick."

"Not bad," I said, walking toward the door.

"Hey, where are you going?"

"The bathroom," I said, not looking back.

"Well, hurry up!" Tom yelled from the conference room, returning to the tone of voice of a boss. "We have to finish this."

I walked down the lonely, dark hallway. Tom and I were the only ones on our floor. The desolate surroundings made the office quite depressing. Everyone else apparently had lives on this Friday night. I looked at my watch, which read 8:10 PM. I shook my head as I entered the restroom. Tom's idea to write a love letter was pretty good. After using the bathroom, I didn't want to forget any of the thoughts that I currently had in my mind. I figured the easiest and quickest thing to do was to leave some of my thoughts on my home answering machine.

I walked into a nearby vacant office and plopped down in the chair. I thought for a moment about what I would say as my eyes scanned the desktop. There were stacks of paperwork, a few files, a calculator, and a snow globe with a small house and a little stick figure farmer inside the globe. I picked up the snow globe, turned it upside-down, and shook it. Snowflakes fluttered everywhere. As I put it down, the small snowflakes floated down over the house and the farmer, which made me smile.

I picked up the phone and dialed the number. The snow in the globe began to settle as I heard the phone ring. I lived alone, so I was waiting for my answering machine to click on. Then, an unbelievable thing happened. Someone picked up the phone and said, "Hello."

I sat straight up in my chair and immediately looked down at the phone display to see if I dialed the correct number. I had. "Hello," the male voice repeated.

I was momentarily stunned as I felt my heartbeat quicken. "I'm sorry. I must have the wrong number. I was trying to reach..." I said before telling him my home phone number.

"You have the right number. Who are you looking for?" the male voice asked. The voice sounded very familiar. My mind was racing and my mouth suddenly became dry. I was speechless, wondering what was going on. Was someone in my house? "Hello! Who are you looking for?" the voice asked again, sounding agitated.

I stammered the only thing I could think of. I asked for myself. "I'm looking for Mark Davidson."

The response was almost too difficult to believe. It was only one word. The voice responded, "Speaking." My eyes widened as I tried to recover from the sense of shock. There wasn't a hint of fear or laughter in the voice. It was said in a matter of fact way.

I quickly gathered myself and recited my address before asking, "Is this the address of this phone number?"

"Who is this?" the voice asked in an angry tone. A sharp chill went up my spine. I recognized the voice. It was mine. In a state of shock, I hastily hung up the phone as if it were a hot plate burning my hand. My heart beat rapidly and my head tilted up toward the ceiling. I slumped back in my chair, moved my head back down, and stared at the phone, trying to comprehend what just happened.

"There you are," Tom said, standing just outside the office door. He motioned with his hand. "Let's go. We..." Tom stopped abruptly. He must have noticed my shocked expression. "What's the matter with you? It looks like you've seen a ghost."

"I may have *heard* one," I said, still staring at the phone. I shook my head, attempting to gather my wits. I turned around in my chair to face Tom at the door. He was obviously confused. I waved him in. "The weirdest thing just happened. I called my house and someone answered, claiming to be me." Tom put his hands on his hips with a perplexed look on his face. "It gets weirder. The voice sounded like me."

"You must have just dialed the wrong number and someone was messing with you." Tom looked down at his watch and pointed at it. "It's 8:15. Shall we get back to work?"

"Hold on," I said, thinking. "We'll call back on the speaker phone, but this time, you'll talk." I motioned for Tom to come over and stand near the phone. Tom sighed and came over as if against his will. "Just ask for me and see if it doesn't sound like me."

I put the speaker phone on and very slowly and carefully dialed my number. The phone rang twice and I waited with anticipation. Shortly after the third ring, someone picked up. It was the same voice. "Hello." It was the same chilling salutation.

Tom hesitated for a moment before speaking loudly into the speaker phone, "May I speak with Mark Davidson please?"

"Speaking," the voice said as Tom and I exchanged glances. I motioned with my hand in small circles to indicate that I wanted him to go on.

"Hi Mark. This is Tom from work."

"Oh hi Tom," the voice said. "How are things going?"

My mouth dropped. It was unbelievable how much the voice sounded like mine.

"I'm fine," Tom said, shrugging his shoulders at me apparently at a loss for words.

"So what's up Tom?" the voice asked, breaking the momentary silence.

I put the speaker phone on mute and quickly said, "Ask him something that a stranger wouldn't know."

Tom nodded and I released the mute button. "Mark, I was calling to tell you that the Wednesday meeting that we had planned got moved up to Monday morning at 8:00 AM in my office. I didn't know if you'd check your voicemail before then so I called you at home."

"No problem," the voice said. "Your office, Monday 8:00 AM. Got it."

"There's one more thing," Tom said as I eyed him. "I saw a memo from you where my name was misspelled. You do know how to spell my last name don't you?"

I gave the crafty Tom a thumbs up sign. "Of course, I do," the voice said after a short pause.

"Spell it for me now then," Tom said.

There was a sigh on the other end of the line before the voice said, "B-R-I-S-E-N." Tom and I looked at each other wide eyed. The voice was right. How could that be? "Is there anything else? I'm kind of in the middle of something here."

"No, that's it," Tom said, clearly in a state of shock. A second later, the voice hung up.

"Is this some kind of joke?" Tom asked.

"No," I said, shaking my head. "I swear. I don't know what's going on. Someone who sounds exactly like me is in my house answering my phone."

"And knows my last name."

"I gotta get home," I said, starting toward the door.

"Hold on a minute. We still have to finish reviewing the purchase agreement."

"I'm sorry, but something strange is going on. I gotta go home."

"Okay, tell you what," Tom said. "It would take at least an hour to get home by the subway. Let me drive you. Then, we can at least talk about the purchase agreement in the car." I just looked at Tom as my mind flashed back to the strange phone calls. "You can ride in my brand new Mercedes." He gestured with his right hand and said, "Speedy, comfortable Mercedes" and then motioned with his left hand, "Slow, smelly subway. So what's it going to be?"

"Alright, alright," I said in deep thought. "But what can I do now about my house?" Tom shrugged his shoulders as I thought about calling the police. The problem was that I wouldn't know what to say without sounding crazy. "I know. I'll call my next-door neighbor."

"Not a bad idea," Tom said, rubbing his chin. "While you do that, I'll pack up and call my wife. Let her know I'm coming home."

After Tom left the room, I sat back in my chair and thought for a moment about what I was going to say to my next-door neighbor, Chris. I decided to keep things simple without going into great detail. My hands were actually shaking a bit as I slowly dialed Chris' phone number. He was somewhere between an acquaintance and a friend. A little too flaky and too spoiled to be a friend, Chris received the house next door as a 25th birthday present from his wealthy parents. I think they felt it was the easiest way to get him out of their house. Still, he was a good guy who seemed to like me a lot. Being away from his family, I think he looked up to me like a big brother.

Chris answered on the third ring. "Hello!" he yelled over the background noise of the television.

I quickly pulled the phone away from my ear, albeit too late. I brought the phone back to my ear. "Hi Chris. It's Mark. I need you to do me a favor. Are you on your portable phone?"

"Yeah," Chris replied in his typical laid-back tone.

"Good, walk over to your side bedroom window, the one that has a clear view of my house."

"Alright." I could tell Chris was walking because the background noise of the television had disappeared. "Okay dude, I'm at the window."

"Now, look in and around my house carefully. Do you see anyone?"

After a short pause, Chris said, "Nah. The house is completely dark." I breathed a sigh of relief. My body relaxed in the chair. "Say, what's this all about?"

"I'll tell you later," I said, looking at my watch. "It's 8:20. Just do me a favor and keep an eye on my house for the next hour. I should be home by then. If you see anything suspicious, call the police. Okay?"

"Sure thing." Just as we hung up, I could hear the television in the background again, which told me he had walked back to his original location.

I impatiently waited as Tom finished his call with his wife and then gathered up all his files. I wanted to yell for him to hurry up, but I didn't want to antagonize my boss, and more importantly, my fastest ticket home. I told Tom about my conversation with Chris, which caused him to say, "I think you're making a big deal out of nothing."

I really didn't know what to think about my phone calls home as I rode in Tom's car, but I knew it was not *nothing*. I looked at the speedometer and saw Tom was going 35 mph on the city streets. "What's the point of having a car like this if you're not going to go faster than this?"

"Hey," Tom said as he stopped for a light, which was clearly on yellow. "I want to be around to enjoy the car, okay."

I declined to get into an argument with him and we spent the rest of the car ride talking about the purchase agreement even though part of my mind was still trying to make sense of my phone calls to my house. "I just don't see it," I said. "If the seller wants this much cash in the transaction, they're going to have to pay some income tax."

"What is it that I've always told you?" Tom said, glancing at me for a second before looking back at the road. "There's always a solution."

"Well, I don't see it."

"That just means we're not looking in the right place," Tom said with a smile.

I scratched my head and I began going over another set of alternatives to structure the purchase. It was about a 40-minute drive (which would have been 30 minutes if I were driving) before I was dropped off at my car at the subway station parking lot.

When Tom pulled next to my car, I turned toward him and asked, "Do you want to come with me? Solve this mystery?"

"No, I'd better go home and finish looking at this agreement. Somebody's got to," Tom said with a smile. I nodded, got out and headed toward my car. The parking lot was barren since almost all the commuters had begun their weekend over three hours ago. I glanced at my watch, which read 9:00. It was a cool, clear night as a full moon lit up the sky. "Mark!" Tom yelled from his my car. "Be careful."

I nodded and he drove away.

It only took ten minutes to get to my house. I slowly pulled up on the side of the street opposite my house. I turned off my car lights. I was stunned to see a gray BMW parked in front of my house. It looked like my fiancée's car. I scratched my head. What the heck was going on here?

I focused my attention on my house. It was completely dark. Just as Chris had told me, nothing appeared out of the ordinary. The neighborhood seemed peaceful with the only sounds being a few crickets in the distance.

I stepped out of my car and felt the brisk cool air. I wished I had my hunting rifle, which unfortunately was stored in my bedroom closet. I opened the trunk where I kept my umbrella. In a pinch, the large, black umbrella could be used as a weapon. I slowly and cautiously crossed the street and walked up my driveway. When I got to the door, I put my ear up to the door. There was dead silence. If anyone had been in my house, it seems as if they were long gone.

I inspected the front door. There were no signs of forced entry. I slowly put the key in the lock and opened the door. As soon as the door was opened, I reached for the nearby light switch. After turning on the light, everything appeared normal in the front hallway.

I breathed a sigh of relief, figuring I had made a big deal out of nothing. I locked the door behind me and walked down the hallway, still holding the umbrella tightly in my right hand. When I turned the corner at the end of the hallway, I stopped in my tracks. I could see a figure lying face down on the dark living room floor. "Who's there?" I said, raising the umbrella with my right hand. There was no answer and the figure didn't move. I fumbled with my left hand, searching for the light switch, all the while keeping both eyes fixed on the figure on the floor.

Finally, I reached the light switch. Once the lights were turned on, I recognized the figure and my mouth dropped in disbelief. It was my fiancée Kirstin. I raced over to her, but stopped short in horror. She lay in a pool of blood with a visible bloody wound in her back. She had been shot. I felt her right wrist for a pulse, but I knew she wouldn't have one.

I stepped back as a stream of tears flowed down as the realization of what happened hit me. The pit of my stomach tightened and I began to feel nauseous. I then swirled around as I began to fear for my own life. I backed into a table as my eyes darted around the room looking for the intruder. I grabbed the portable phone on the living room table, before racing back down the hallway and out the front door. From the sidewalk, I called the police, frantically telling them there had been a murder in my house. Then, I rushed next door and anxiously rang the door bell several times, periodically yelling out

"Chris!" Every few seconds I'd look back over my shoulder to make sure no one was exiting my house.

Chris' porch light came on, momentarily blinding me. "Dude! What's going on?" Chris asked, opening the door. He was wearing blue jeans and a long sleeve blue shirt that was not tucked in. His full head of hair seemed unusually unkempt as he stuck his head outside trying to figure out what was going on.

I motioned with my hand. "I need you! Come on. Quick!" We raced across the street and got in my car and looked at my house from across the street.

"You mind telling me what's going on?" Chris asked me as he sat in the passenger seat of my car.

"Someone broke into my house and murdered Kirstin," I said, glancing at Chris.

Chris gasped and put his hand over his heart.

I focused my eyes back on the house. "I just called the police and the killer may still be in the house." My heart and emotions were going a mile a minute. "I'm going to run him down if he comes out. I needed some backup." I turned to Chris who seemed to be in shock with the news I had just laid on him. I looked at him and said, "You're my backup." Chris began to nervously run his hands through his hair. "Say," I said, trying to get him to focus. "After I called, did you observe anything unusual? See anyone enter the house?"

There was a momentary silence before Chris said, "I'm sorry. I... I... uh, was watching this movie on TV and really didn't pay that much attention."

I fought the temptation to get upset or even look at him. I exhaled audibly as I looked at Kirstin's car in front of my house. "How about Kirstin's car? Was it here when I called?"

Chris squinted as if he was trying to make himself remember. "When I was on the phone with you, I really wasn't looking at the street. I was really more focused on the house. I can't be sure."

Just as Chris was finishing his sentence, I saw flashing lights approaching in my rear view mirror. We got out of the car and crossed the street.

The police car pulled up to the driveway. A pair of officers jumped out of the car and immediately approached us. I quickly explained what happened. A few moments later, two other squad cars with flashing lights arrived. With guns drawn, they circled the home outside before searching inside. I waited outside with Chris, hoping the officer would catch the intruder who may have been cowering in one of my closets.

There was no such luck. About ten minutes later, the group of officers emerged from the house empty handed. An officer pulled me away from Chris announcing that he wanted to ask me a few questions. I looked back over my shoulder and noticed that another officer was about to do the same with Chris.

The officer asked me to step around toward the back of a squad car. A number of my neighbors stood outside on their porches wondering what was going on. The flashing lights of the three patrol cars had obviously gotten their attention in this quiet, suburban neighborhood.

The officer asked me some very basic questions related to the circumstances of how I found the body and my relationship with the deceased. I briefly mentioned the voice I heard when I called my house. The police officer wanted to know more details, but my mind started spinning. I was having difficulty answering the simplest of questions. I felt lightheaded and had to sit down in the patrol car. My mind kept flashing back to the sight of Kirstin's murdered body and I began to get physically ill. The officer, realizing my condition, instructed me to lie down at Chris' house. He mentioned that someone in the department would contact me very soon.

That night I stayed over at Chris' house because the police restricted access to my house. I was so tired physically and emotionally, I fell asleep very quickly. I had a dream that Kirstin and I were hiking and she fell off the side of the mountain. Right after she left my view and disappeared over the side of the mountain, I awoke in a cold sweat.

I shot up in bed and wiped my forehead. I was breathing hard and momentarily wondered if everything over the last 24 hours was a dream. Then reality hit. I swallowed hard as I realized I was sleeping in Chris' guest bedroom. It was no dream. It was very real. Tears joined the perspiration on my face as I realized that I would never hold Kirstin in my arms again.

The police contacted me that morning. They asked me to come down to the station at 3:00 PM for further questions. I decided to call Sam, a defense lawyer who had been practicing over 25 years. It was the first time that I had ever been formally questioned by the police in my life. I knew I'd feel better with him on my side.

Sam, a close college friend of my father's, has been like family my entire life. He had a charismatic personality and was always spending time telling a mystical story or showing an amazing trick. Sam was both creative and smart. And most importantly, I knew I could trust him.

That morning I called Sam. Over the phone, I told him that Kirstin was murdered in my home and the police had called me down to the station for formal questioning. The phone line went silent for a few seconds before Sam said, "My God, Kirstin was murdered! Are you okay?"

"I'm okay. I'm a little nervous about going down to the police station."

"You did the right thing by calling me," Sam said, which made me feel better. "Let's meet for lunch and then we'll go over to the station together," Sam said before suggesting a place and time for lunch.

"The café on Mission Street, 12 noon today. Got it," I said before hanging up.

An hour and a half later, I was sitting at a table across from Sam. The café was small and we had a table in the corner so it was pretty quiet. Sam ordered a full lunch, but I just ordered a soda because I was too nervous and anxious to eat.

Sam had a full head of black hair, which was slicked back. He wore small, stylish round glasses that accented his clean-shaven face. Sam was always impeccably neat when it came to his appearance. "Perception is 9/10 of reality" was his favorite phrase over the years. If Sam had a flaw, it would be his lack of tact. A self-proclaimed straight shooter, Sam didn't mince words when he felt strongly about something.

"I have a question to ask you before we start," Sam said. He leaned forward. "It doesn't matter what your answer is. What's important is that it's the truth. Understand?" I answered with a nod, looking at him straight in the eye. Sam tilted his head as he whispered, "Did you have anything to do with Kirstin's death?"

My eyes widened with the question. "Of course not."

"Good," Sam said, sitting back in his chair before I walked Sam through my entire day, including the eerie phone calls. Sam listened intently, rarely interrupting, pausing occasionally to jot down some notes.

"Well, you have an alibi for the entire night. That's good," Sam said before taking a sip of his iced tea. Instinctively, I drank from my soda. I welcomed the change that the cool, carbonated soda made to my previously dry mouth. "The problem is if the police believe that you met Kirstin at your house and killed her right before calling them." I fumed inside at the notion that the police would suspect me of murdering Kirstin. I remained tight-lipped as I simmered with frustration and anger, balling my left hand up in a fist. "But don't you worry about that," Sam said tapping my left hand. "All you have to do is tell the truth to the police as confidently as you just did to me and everything will be okay."

Two hours later, Sam and I were escorted into a small room at the police station. A detective named Bud Davis introduced himself with a firm handshake, before saying, "Please, call me Bud." Bud introduced his partner, but Bud indicated that he was heading the investigation and leading today's questioning. Bud was of average height with a noticeable gut. He had a receding hairline and a bushy mustache. As I sat down, he smiled which put me a little at ease.

"This will be a simple and short interview. We're just on a fact finding mission today to get as much information as we can so we can catch the perpetrator of this crime."

"I'd like nothing more than to have the person responsible for Kirstin's death brought to justice," I said, clasping my hands together and resting them on the table.

"Good," Bud said, pulling out a file and putting on some reading glasses. "Let's start by confirming some things about your background." Bud asked a series of innocuous questions regarding my birth date, address, educational background, hobbies, and occupation. "The officer on duty last night mentioned you were working late that night. Is that correct?"

"Yes, that's correct."

"Can you account for your whereabouts that night?"

"Well, yeah," I said with a slight nod. "I was in my office building in the city from 1:30 through around 8:15. And except for a few minutes during that time frame, I was with my boss Tom Brisen the entire time working together in a conference room. He drove me to the subway station, which took about 40 minutes. I remember getting to the station at about 9:00. I drove straight home from the subway station. That's a ten minute ride. I discovered her body shortly after I arrived at my house."

"Good," Bud said with a smirk. I'm guessing his expression was caused by the completeness of my answer. I wondered if my answer sounded rehearsed. "Tell me how you discovered the body."

"Well, when I got home, I unlocked the front door, came down the hallway, and I saw…" I paused as I put my left hand up to my forehead as I suddenly felt a swell of emotions. I was reliving the gory scene of discovering Kirstin's body in my mind as I rubbed the bridge of my nose and squinted. The room was silent as I knew all eyes were on me. I somehow gathered myself and I took a deep breath before finishing my sentence. I said slowly and forcefully, "I saw Kirstin dead on the floor." I paused a moment before quickly saying, "I called the police immediately."

Bud scribbled notes on his pad of paper. I took this opportunity to wipe a tear from my right eye. Sam patted me on the back as if to remind me that he was there. "According to my notes, your fiancée, Kirstin Wesley, did not live with you. Is that correct?"

"No… no she didn't live with me."

"Did she have a key to your house?"

I paused a bit before shaking my head and saying at the same time, "No she didn't." Bud had a perplexed look on his face. "What?"

"Well," Bud said. "If Kirstin didn't live with you and she didn't have a key, how did she get into the house if you weren't home?"

"That, I don't know for sure," I said.

Bud nodded before asking, "When was the last time that you talked to your fiancée?"

"About 5:30 last night. I called her to cancel our plans that night and rescheduled for the following night."

"Did she seem worried, frightened, or act unusual at all?"

I paused a moment, remembering Sam's warning not to go into too much detail. "No, not really."

"Do you know what she was planning to do that night since you had canceled your plans?"

"No," I said, shaking my head for emphasis. "She was home with her roommate Cathy. Perhaps she could tell you more. I know Cathy was home because she answered the phone when I called."

There was a pause as both Bud and his partner scribbled some notes.

"Now, a minute ago, you said you called to cancel your plans, but the one thing we know for sure is that she drove over to your house last night. Why would she do that when you cancelled your plans?"

I shrugged my shoulders. "I don't have the faintest idea."

"Do you know anyone who might have wanted to kill Kirstin?" Bud asked bluntly.

"No," I immediately said. "No one."

'Well, who did Kirstin spend most of her free time with?"

"Me, of course. She's also good friends with her roommate, Cathy. They spend a lot of time together."

"How about her family?"

"Kirstin's father died when she was a baby," I said. "Her mother remarried a widowed man. It's obvious that her mother and stepfather love her very much." My mind flashed back to Kirstin's parents. For prospective in-laws, they were pretty good. I liked Kirstin's mother a lot. She had already welcomed me into their family. Kirstin's stepfather on the other hand, had been slow to warm up to me. I think that he worried that I might be trying to marry into their family for the money.

"Her brother, he lives in town as well, right?" Bud said, breaking my concentration.

"A stepbrother. His name is Brian. He's Mr. Wesley's son from a previous marriage."

"What was Kirstin and Brian's relationship like?" Bud asked.

"Kirstin and Brian are very different," I said with a sigh. "They don't see eye to eye on much at all. They..."

"On what, for example?"

"Everything. Money, politics, my hunting, our relationship."

"So, Brian didn't really like you too much?"

I smiled a bit at Bud's summation. "I don't think it's anything personal. I think he's just trying to look out for his kid sister, you know."

"But, lately, it doesn't sound like Brian and Kirstin had gotten along too well," Bud surmised.

"Brian didn't kill his sister," I said, realizing Bud's train of thought. "Even though she was a step sister, they grew up together in the same house. Brian really did love his sister. Now that she was getting older, he just had a funny way of showing it."

"The officer on duty said you called your house that night," Bud said, changing the subject. We discussed the exact time that I called, the reason why I called home, and the conversation to the best of my recollection. "There were no visible signs of forced entry. How do you suppose this person would have gotten into your house?"

"I've no idea. You know, I'd like to make the point that the voice sounded exactly like mine. You can talk to Tom Brisen, my boss. He heard it as well."

"Hmmm," Bud said, thinking. "The whole phone call seems...what's the word I'm trying to think of...just very odd." Bud raised his eyebrows as an invitation to me to speak. I decided to remain silent. "You know, like something right out of a Twilight Zone episode." I nodded uncomfortably in response to his words. The questioning continued for another fifteen minutes before the interview was completed.

Sam congratulated me, stating that I did a good job. "Soon," Sam said, patting me on the back. "This will all be over."

I checked my voicemail and received a message from Tom. He mentioned that he heard about Kirstin's death when the police contacted him. He expressed his deepest sympathies and said, "Take as much time off as you need." It was an emotional lift knowing that I didn't need to think about work.

The next few days were tough. Kirstin's funeral was on Wednesday. The bright sunshine and clear day belied the horrible reality. The love of my life was ripped away from me, viciously and apparently senselessly. My emotions shifted regularly between depression and anger. But, one thing was certain: a part of me died with her.

After the services at the mortuary, I had an opportunity to talk to Kirstin's parents. They looked more advanced in age than you would expect. In their early sixties, they both seemed to have aged greatly in the last couple of days.

"This is such a sad day," Mrs. Wesley said. A beautiful diamond necklace was draped across her neck. The wind picked up a bit and Mrs. Wesley put her hand over her black hat to make sure it wasn't blown away. The tall Mr. Wesley squeezed his wife. I'm not sure for comfort or support. Mr. Wesley had a squarish face that conveyed a stern, intimidating presence. Mrs. Wesley continued, looking directly at me, "No one could be more heartbroken than you dear. How are you holding up?"

"It's been tough, but somehow I'm holding it together."

Mr. Wesley's white hair swayed in the wind. Dressed in a well-tailored black suit, he squinted a bit at my direction before saying, "I suppose you feel lucky that you weren't with her when she was shot in your own house."

"In a way, yes," I replied before pausing to make sure my answer was not insensitive. "But, I can't help thinking that I could have stopped it."

Mr. Wesley nodded his head slightly, apparently in deep thought.

"What type of person would do such a horrible thing?" Mrs. Wesley said, visibly shaking. She closed her eyes and put her left hand over her heart.

"A sick person," Mr. Wesley said. "A very sick person."

"Hey! What are you doing?" a voice said from behind me. I turned around and saw it was Brian. I always felt Brian was a spoiled brat. He got most of his things in life handed to him by his dear old dad. It wasn't that I was jealous. I mean, I like my next door neighbor Chris who I thought was spoiled. But, Brian was nothing like Chris. Brian was ungrateful and mean spirited. Because his family had a lot of money, Brian thought he was better than other people. Despite his pretty boy good looks, his attitude always made him look like an ogre to me. He stuck his finger near my face and said, "You stay away from my family!"

"Brian dear," Mrs. Wesley said, stepping in between the two of us. "We were having a pleasant conversation. You know, we're all suffering with the loss of Kirstin."

"Uh huh," Brian said, looking over his mother at me. Brian always liked to pretend that he was a tough guy. In the past, he claimed that he was "protecting" Kirstin from me. He liked to talk tough, but unlike his father, Brian didn't intimidate. Despite the fact that we were the same height and build, I knew I could take him if an altercation ever became physical. But, it never did. Brian was all bark and no bite.

Brian said, "I won't rest until I find out who killed my little sister." He gestured toward me over his mother's shoulder. "And you'd better hope you didn't have anything to do with it."

"Brian!" Mrs. Wesley shouted. "How dare you say such a thing?"

"I'm watching you," Brian said, pointing his finger at me again before leaving.

Shortly after the unpleasant conversation with Brian, the group of mourners walked to the burial site. As they lowered Kirstin's casket into the ground, I lost it emotionally. Streams of tears flowed down my cheeks as I sobbed. I fell down to my knees as the realization hit me deep down that I would never see Kirstin again.

Once the burial ceremony was over, I had regained a little bit of composure. Taking deep breaths repeatedly became very important. As the crowd slowly departed the grave site, I noticed Cathy starting to walk back toward the mortuary alone. I had gotten to know her pretty well over the last two years. As Kirstin's closest friend, she had to be suffering too.

I put my hand on her shoulder. A steady breeze was blowing her long red hair, which was draped down past her shoulders. Cathy immediately turned around. Her eyes were red, likely from the many tears she had shed during the day. When she noticed it was me, a disgusted look crossed her pretty face. "G..get your hands off me," Cathy said, moving her shoulder away as she started to sob.

"What's the matter with you?"

"Just stay away from me, okay," Cathy said as she backed away. She pulled out several tissues and began to wipe tears from her eyes.

"No! What's the problem? Tell me."

"I know you killed Kirstin," Cathy said as she sniffled. "I know it." She began briskly walking away.

"What are you talking about?!" I yelled. But, she didn't stop and I chose not to go after her.

No amount of stress or emotional impact that the funeral brought could prepare me for what happened Thursday morning.

Inspector Bud Davis came by, accompanied by several uniformed officers. I answered the door, still unsure what was going on. Then, the words came, "You're under arrest." The rest was a blur. I'm pretty sure I heard my Miranda Rights being read. In a daze, I was led to a police car and driven to the police station.

At the police station, an officer took my fingerprints and picture. It was an unreal experience, like a very bad dream. I was allowed to call Sam, who told me to keep calm. Now that I was arrested, Sam told me he would gain access to all of the police's evidence. He said he wanted to go over that evidence and he would come to see me as soon as possible. He had an admonition for me that was very clear, "Say absolutely nothing to anyone until I arrive."

I remained in a holding cell for the next four hours alone with my thoughts. I thought about the snow globe and the farmer who stood outside his house. One moment, his world was normal as he went about his day. Then, it was violently shaken up. I felt like that farmer. My world was turned upside-down. The problem was that the snow in my life continued to fall on me with no end in sight.

Sam met me in a small room in the police station. We were alone in the room, but an officer stood just outside the door. I embraced Sam, happy to have some human contact. "How you holding up?"

"I've been better," I said as I sat down.

"Well, I have good news and I've got bad news," Sam said, pulling out several sheets of paper from his briefcase. I rubbed my face in nervous anticipation. "First, the good news. The autopsy showed that Kirstin died between an hour and a half and three and a half hours before the police arrived on the scene. That means you couldn't have killed her right before you called the police."

"That *is* great news," I said. "I've got an alibi for the rest of the night. I was with Tom during that whole time." Sam had his head down, looking at the ground. There was an uncomfortable silence in the room. "What's the problem?"

"According to this," Sam said, gesturing toward the sheet of paper. "Tom says you left the office around 5:30 and he never saw you after that." My jaw dropped in complete shock. "Wha.. what did you say? I must not have heard you," I said, tilting my head and moving it closer to Sam.

"I said Tom denies you were with him after 5:30 that night. That means you don't have an alibi between six and eight pm, the time that they suspect Kirstin was murdered." I simply shook my head in disbelief. "Worse still, Cathy, Kirstin's roommate, swears that you called to talk to Kirstin right before 5:30."

"Yeah, I called to cancel the plans," I said with my heart pounding against my chest.

"Well, Cathy says you called twice," Sam said, looking down at some paperwork. "The first call was about 5:30 to cancel your plans. The second call was around 6:20 and that was supposedly to put the plans back on."

"That's not true."

"Well, Cathy swears it is," Sam said, holding up a sheet of paper. "Cathy says she answered the phone on both of your calls. The second time she says she handed the phone over to Kirstin and you told Kirstin you were at home." Images flew through my mind as I squeezed my eyes shut and dropped my head wishing I were a million miles away. Undaunted, Sam continued, "Phone records from your house to Cathy's that night support what Cathy claims. The police believe your phone call is why Kirstin came to your house."

"Because I invited her? This is crazy! Why are these people lying?"

"I was hoping you'd be able to tell me that," Sam said, taking off his glasses.

I ran my hands through my hair in sheer frustration as Sam rubbed his eyes. "They can't build a case on the lies of a couple of people, can they?"

"They do have some physical evidence," Sam said, putting his glasses back on.

"What physical evidence?"

"They have determined the bullet that killed Kirstin came from your rifle, which has only your fingerprints."

"I don't lock up my rifle. It was in my closet. Whoever was in my house could have stolen it." I thought for a moment before saying, "And the killer could have worn gloves."

"True." Sam paused to look at the sheet of paper in his hand. He tapped the paper and said, "Says here your work phone that night shows no calls to your home as you claim."

I scratched my head as I felt momentarily confused. I snapped my fingers. "That's because I called from another office. It was the outside office closest to the bathroom."

"Good, that's easily explained," Sam said. "I'll check the phone records for that office, but Tom and Cathy's comments are what really worry me. We have to understand why they're saying what they're saying."

"You talk to Cathy, but *I* need to talk to Tom one on one. I want to challenge him about what he told the police, but I need you to get him down here."

"I don't know if that is such a good…"

"I know I was with him. I can't get to the truth without talking to him."

I had convinced Sam, who promised to get in touch with Tom and to talk to Cathy. He said that tomorrow morning we would be in court in an attempt to get bail posted. "Just hang tough and I'll be in touch," Sam said, giving me a firm handshake before leaving.

About two hours later, a police officer came to my holding cell saying simply, "You've got a visitor." As the officer led me to a small room in the police station, I thought my visitor was Sam, back to give me a status update on his calls to Cathy and Tom. I stopped at the doorway at the sight of the person sitting at the small table. It was Tom.

"I came as soon as I could," Tom said, rising from his chair. The officer gave me a slight push and I walked into the room. A moment later, the door slammed shut as Tom and I were locked in. I glared at Tom, not knowing how I should feel about him. I slowly and methodically walked over to the table and took a seat.

"I can't believe they arrested you," Tom said, looking me straight in the eye. "Listen to me. Anything that I can do to help, you let me know."

I didn't know how to begin. I decided to take the indirect approach. "Tom, the Petersen's purchase agreement. Do you remember that we reviewed that together last Friday?"

"Sure I do," Tom said with a puzzled look on his face.

"Do you remember what time we started working in the conference room that day?"

"Gosh, I don't know. It was just after lunch. Must have been about one or one thirty."

"That's right, and we worked on that agreement together in the conference until eight o'clock."

Tom's forehead wrinkled as he stared at me for a moment. "No," Tom said slowly. "You left around 5:30. You told me that you had to go home and see Kirstin."

"No!" I said, shaking my head as my heart rate quickened. "At about 5:30, you told me we would have to stay late and I had to cancel my plans with Kirstin."

"Well, yeah. I did tell you that, and you did call Kirstin. But then you came back to the conference room and told me how upset Kirstin was." I listened closely and watched Tom carefully. He was calm, relaxed and confident as he talked. He continued, "After you told me how upset Kirstin was and that you were planning to celebrate an anniversary, I told you to go home. And you left."

"What are you talking about? I didn't leave. I stayed in the conference room with you until after eight o'clock." Tom stared at me, searching for words to say. "You drove me home! You have to remember that?"

Tom dropped his head and his eyes shifted up to look at me. He stared at me as if I were crazy. "Mark, I stayed in the office until about 8:30 reviewing the agreement, but I was alone. And I drove home alone."

I clasped my hands together and rested them behind my head as I leaned back in my chair. I couldn't believe what was happening. "What about the phone call we made to my house?" I said. Tom tilted his head to the side and looked at me with a confused look on his face. "Come on!" I said in frustration as I balled up my hands into tight fists. "You must remember the phone call with the person who sounded just like me."

Tom took a deep breath and exhaled slowly. "I don't know what you're talking about. I don't remember any phone call to your house." I glared at Tom, trying to contain my anger and frustration. I decided to remain quiet for a moment until I calmed down a bit. "What's this all about? Is this about you having an alibi?" I remained silent staring at the table. "Look, Mark, I want to help you out of this mess, but I can't lie."

"I'm not asking you to lie!" I shouted, pounding both fists on the table. Tom became wide eyed as he fell back in his chair.

"Hey!" a voice yelled. Tom and I quickly looked up at the police officer who had just entered the room. "What's the problem?"

"There's no problem," Tom quickly responded as he held his left arm in the air.

"No problem," I said, embarrassed with my outburst.

"Well, keep it down in here," the officer said before leaving and closing the door behind him.

"Sorry about that." Tom nodded to acknowledge that he accepted my apology. "But Tom, I swear to you. I'm not lying. What I am telling you is we worked in that conference room together until after eight o'clock and then you drove me home. You don't remember that?"

"That's not my memory," Tom said, shaking his head. "And you know I would help you with an alibi if I could."

"This doesn't make sense," I said, scratching my head. "How can we have completely different memories of what happened that night?"

Tom and I just looked at the ground for what seemed like 30 seconds without saying a word. Tom finally said, "There has to be a rational explanation for all this. Some logical solution."

I looked at Tom and said in deep thought, "It's like you always say. We must not be looking in the right place."

I spent the next 24 hours in a cell buried in books. Tom had brought back from the library any book he could find on paranormal events. My research told me a parallel universe could be triggered by an atmospheric event. Once triggered, two different realities can be experienced because a separate, mysterious, and sometimes opposite world becomes intertwined with ours. Similar surroundings and people inhabit the parallel universe, but completely different events, caused by different motivations by its inhabitants, take place. I found it weird to be pouring over this type of research. Although I have always been a big fan of science fiction, I never believed such things could actually happen. But, it's amazing what you'll do when desperation sets in. It's like a sick man who seeks alternative methods when modern conventional medicine fails. Be it potions, herbs, or magical oils, the sick man will leave no stone unturned to save his life.

Similarly, I was trying to save my life with the pending trial. I was hoping to find some answers through cases, any cases, of strange occurrences that resembled mine. If there was one fact that proved my situation was very abnormal, it was the voice on that phone call. It sounded like me. It sounded *exactly* like me. The voice inflection was just like mine. The words and phrases were the same as I would use. I was convinced, as unbelievable as it was, that the voice was mine. I believed that I crossed paths with an evil version of myself from a parallel universe!

Also furthering this mysterious belief was the fact that Tom and I somehow experienced two alternative realities that night. I trusted Tom. There's no way he would lie about this. There would be no reason for him to.

The next day was a successful one in court. After pleading not guilty, I made bail. I was a free man, for the time being. Over the next couple of days, I continued my search into the supernatural.

Sam seemed annoyed with my preoccupation with such matters. While I read books that explored unexplained occurrences and parallel universes, Sam reviewed the prosecution's evidence again. "Maybe, we ought to give you a psychiatric exam and see if we can use the insanity defense," Sam said snidely from across the room.

"Sam," I said, taking a deep breath. "I'm sure something very abnormal happened that night. I really think it may have something to do with a parallel universe."

"Even if that were true, which it isn't. We can't go to the jury with a defense of a parallel universe."

I shook my head at Sam before burying my head back in another book. Sam didn't seem to get it. I had to figure out what happened. And the world as I know it didn't provide any answers.

The next day, my next door neighbor Chris came over to see how I was holding up. I took the opportunity to explain to him, in detail, the events that happened the night of Kirstin's death. I expected that he'd lend a more sympathetic ear than Sam regarding my parallel universe theory.

"That's pretty far out there, dude," Chris said, proving my prediction erroneous.

"It may be, but I can't think of any other explanation. I mean, I know I was in that office with Tom and I never called Kirstin back to say we were going to meet that night. But, Tom and Cathy swear that's not true. Can you explain that?"

Chris scratched his head before saying, "Well, as a matter of fact, I do have an idea."

"You do?" I sat up in my chair. He had my complete attention.

"I'm just throwing this out there," Chris said, holding both hands up as he leaned back in his chair. "I'm not saying this is necessarily the case, okay?"

I closed my eyes, growing frustrated. "Just tell me."

"I saw this special on TV once about multiple personalities. The guy had all these different personalities and one couldn't remember some of the stuff the others had done. It was pretty cool. One personality was a Broadway singer and he didn't even know how to…"

"Look Chris," I said, shaking my head. "I don't have multiple personalities, alright."

"Sure, whatever, but let me say one thing. You seem so sure you don't have multiple personalities." I nodded my head with assurance. "Well, that's what the guy on TV thought too."

After Chris left, I thought more about our conversation. I'm not sure why I dismissed Chris' suggestion of multiple personalities so quickly while I clung to the admittedly bizarre parallel universe theory. I think the reason was simple. I could never believe that any part of me could be responsible for taking Kirstin's life.

The days before the trial flew by. Before I knew it, two weeks had passed and I was back in court. Sam convinced me that our best defense strategy was to attack the prosecution's case and avoid discussing where I was that night. My relationship with Kirstin's family soured further after my arrest. They would not return my phone calls. Even Mrs. Wesley, who had always liked me, had not contacted me. When the trial began, Mr. and Mrs. Wesley, and Brian sat right behind the prosecution's table, indicating where their loyalties lay.

When I saw them in court, Mrs. Wesley seemed very distraught, possibly having many mixed emotions about the day. Mr. Wesley held onto his wife tightly, focused on getting her through this ordeal. Mr. Wesley glared at me with hatred in his eyes. Brian, on the other hand, had a smirk on his face. He seemed happy about the predicament that I was in, and possibly even happier that he was there to witness it.

I'm not sure how I expected the trial to go, but it clearly was worse than I had anticipated. From the beginning, the prosecution came out firing. Sam had warned me that the district attorney's office assigned one of their best attorneys to the case. Her name was Alicia Silver. I quickly realized she was articulate, energetic and very passionate.

During opening statements, Alicia painted me as a jealous, controlling creep who killed Kirstin when she threatened to break-up with me. She arrogantly challenged me saying, "You watch, ladies and gentleman of the jury, the defendant will provide no evidence for where he was during this despicable murder. The defense will provide no evidence." Alicia made a circle with her thumb and index finger and said loudly, "None!" She ended dramatically saying, "And that's because the only evidence says he was in his own house at that time murdering his fiancée who had threatened to break up with him." Alicia paused, raising her index finger and pointing directly at me saying, "If the defendant couldn't have her, he made darn sure no one else could."

Both Mr. Wesley and Brian testified on the prosecution's behalf, saying everything that the prosecution wanted. Each gave instances where they claimed I was controlling and each testified that Kirstin had talked to them about doubts about the upcoming marriage. Brian went as far as to say that Kirstin told him a week ago that she was considering calling off the wedding.

It was unbelievable. It was as if they were describing someone else. They were taking everything out of context. It was maddening to have to sit quietly and watch them testify. Sam did an admirable job of cross-examining them, but I was unsure what the jury would believe. I could feel some of them looking at me differently now. My palms got sweaty and my heart rate soared whenever I thought about how much was at stake in this trial.

After setting up the motive, the prosecution went straight to opportunity. They called Cathy to the stand. "The night Kirstin was murdered. Do you know what her original plans were?" Alicia asked.

"I do, "Cathy said. "I was with her that evening. She was going over to Mark's house for dinner."

"Did her plans ever change?"

"Well, yes. At 5:30, Mark called to cancel the plans. He said he had to work late."

"How did Kirstin take the cancellation?" Alicia asked.

"Oh, she was livid. It was the third time in a row he had cancelled because of work. They had a heated phone conversation."

"You overheard it?"

"Hard not to. Besides, Kirstin told me all about it after she got off."

"So, she just stayed home for the night?"

"No," Cathy said, shaking her head. "About an hour later, Mark calls back and says…"

"Hold on a minute. How do you know he called back?"

"I answered the phone. I know his voice. He asked to speak to Kirstin. He told her he was sorry and that he got out of working late. He was already home and wanted her to come over. She left between 6:45 and 7:00 to go over there. And that's the last time I ever saw her."

Alicia dipped her head before saying she had no further questions. Sam did his best during cross examination, but I felt that the damage had already been done.

The prosecution then called a police officer to testify that my house showed no signs of a break in. Alicia argued that only I would have access to my house. Only I could be the killer because Kirstin wouldn't enter my house without me being there. Kirstin didn't have a key.

The prosecution then brought an expert to prove that the bullet likely came from a rifle like mine. The expert went on to claim that my rifle was fired that night and the only fingerprints on that rifle were mine.

The prosecution rested at the end of the second day. That night, I met with Sam at my house. Sam was pouring over court transcripts at a table as I sat on the sofa across the room. "We're getting killed. I have to testify."

"No," Sam said, looking up from his work. "We've gone over this. You can't testify." Sam pointed his pencil at me to drive home his point. "If you testify, the prosecution can ask you where you were that night. When you say you were at work, they'll call Tom to completely refute it."

"Well, I can't just sit there and say nothing," I argued. "Remember what the prosecution said in opening statements.

They told the jury we wouldn't provide evidence of my whereabouts. The jury will at least want to hear me say I didn't do it."

"You already did that when you plead not guilty," Sam said, adjusting his glasses higher up the bridge of his nose. "Our only defense is character witnesses. We'll put people up there to say that you never have committed a crime in your life and how loving you were toward Kirstin. I thought we'd lead off with your next door neighbor Chris."

"No. That won't be good enough." I slowly rose and crossed my arms in front of my chest. "I've decided. I'm taking the stand."

"And then what?" Sam said, getting up from his chair. He walked over to me and looked at me dead in the eye. "When they totally refute your alibi with Tom's testimony, then what?"

There was an uncomfortable pause as I stared back at Sam's intense face. "Then we bring up parallel universes. It's the only possible explanation."

"Ack!!" Sam said, throwing his hands in the air. He turned, walking a few paces away with both hands on his hips. He swirled around. "Are you crazy? We're not bringing up parallel universes in a court of law. You'll be put away for sure."

"If I say nothing, I'll be found guilty for sure too. I might as well go with the truth."

Sam groaned and covered his face in frustration. "There's one other possibility," Sam said with his face still covered.

"What?"

Sam removed his hands from his face and said solemnly, "You can see if the prosecution will plea bargain." I sighed audibly and Sam wagged his index finger saying, "It's something to consider. They might go for second-degree murder and fifteen years."

"No," I said, shaking my head furiously. "I'm not taking a plea. I didn't do anything wrong."

Sam and I looked at each other for a while in complete silence. The incomprehensible thought of fifteen years in prison was flashing through my mind when Sam said, "So where does this leave us?"

"Look, you figure the courtroom strategy," I said, walking past Sam toward the closet. "I'm going to try something." I opened the closet door and put on my coat.

"Where are you going?"

"I'll be back in less than an hour." I raced out the door leaving a confused, agitated Sam behind.

I pulled my car up to Tom Brisen's house. I slowly got out of my car and walked up the driveway. I had my right hand in my coat pocket, caressing my last hope for freedom. It was a long shot, but for now, it was my only shot. I rang the doorbell.

The door was thrust open and Tom looked stunned. "Mark!" He motioned with his hand. "Please, come in."

We sat down in the living room. Tom explained that his wife had just left to pick up some things at the grocery store. "Want something to drink?"

"No thanks," I said, deciding to get right to the point. I pulled a sheet of paper from my jacket pocket and handed it Tom.

Tom had a confused look on his face as he took the paper from me. He reached into his pocket and pulled out his reading glasses. As Tom read it, my stomach was filled with butterflies. I took short, quick breaths to make sure air made it into my lungs.

"Very nice," Tom said nodding. "Very well written." Tom handed the letter back to me and put his glasses back in his pocket. My heart dropped in sorrow. So far, it hadn't worked. I decided to remain silent and hope. "It was still a good idea," Tom finally said.

"Excuse me? What did you say?"

"Well, that was a love letter to Kirstin," Tom said, gesturing at the sheet of paper. "I'm the one who suggested that idea. Admit it. That was a good idea."

I fell back on the sofa and felt a rush of emotions. Relief. Excitement. Anger. "You're right. You did suggest that. You suggested it to me in the office that Friday night at about eight o'clock."

"No," Tom said, shifting in his seat. "It was that day, but it was much earlier, like about five o'clock."

"Couldn't be. The whole reason that you suggested it to me was because I couldn't go home. The note was to make up for missing the date. The fact that you remember telling me to write this note proves that you knew I didn't leave at 5:30 like you told the police. You had to know that I stayed late, missing our date."

Tom fell back in his chair and looked to the ceiling as if he were searching for a way out of this. I said, "This didn't have anything to do with parallel universes or multiple personalities. You and I were both in the same conference room at eight o'clock. And you were with me when I called home and heard that voice." Tom remained silent just looking at the ceiling. "Look, I don't know why you lied. And right now, I don't even care. I just need you to come testify in court supporting my alibi." Tom finally looked away from the ceiling and turned toward me, but still remained silent. "Tom!" I said, raising my voice. "We're talking about my life here."

"If I do that, I'm a dead man," Tom said.

"A dead man. Why?"

"I've worked on the Wesley account for over fifteen years. Let me put it this way. Not everything they do is on the up and up."

"What are you talking about?"

"And there's no one who has their hands dirtier than good ol' Mr. Wesley," Tom said with a nervous chuckle. "Mr. Wesley called me on the phone and said it's essential that I keep you late in the office that Friday night. He didn't say why, just said he'd wire me $10,000. Then, he made me promise that we never had that conversation." I stayed silent in complete shock about what I was hearing and just let Tom continue to talk. "I had no idea what he was planning. I guessed it had something to do with trying to break up you and Kirstin." Tom tilted his head and said bluntly, "Mr. Wesley never trusted you."

"I don't understand," I said. "This doesn't explain why you lied about not being with me that night."

"I didn't tell you about the second call yet. Mr. Wesley called me again at my house late that Friday night. He told me the following things." Tom stuck his right hand in the air and began counting on his fingers. "First, you called Kirstin twice that night, once to cancel the plans and then once to put the plans back on. Second, you had left the office at about 5:30 to meet Kirstin. I insisted that you were with me in the office until 8:20 when I drove you home, but he made it *clear* that you left at 5:30, not 8:20. He said that he'd wire me another $10,000 and warned me never to change my story because he needed it to protect himself. Mark, I swear I had no idea Kirstin's life was ever in any danger."

"So, you think Mr. Wesley murdered Kirstin?"

"I know it. He called me the day after Kirstin's death to tell me that Kirstin died and reminded me to keep to our story. When I asked him why, he came out and admitted it."

"Admitted what?" I asked, leaning forward on the sofa.

"Murdering her," Tom replied.

I ran my hands through my hair. "What did you say to him?"

"Nothing, I was speechless. Mr. Wesley ended the conversation by saying that he never wanted to discuss this again. I remember his tone. He was deadly serious."

"I can't believe this," I said, shaking my head.

"Mr. Wesley has been mixed up with some bad people for a long time. Now, I know this because I handled his account over the years. He has had his hands deep into everything. Drug smuggling, professional hits, you name it."

"I need you to come to court and say all this," I said.

"If I have a death wish, I could just drink cyanide."

"I can have you subpoenaed to testify."

"That will only hurt you if I repeat my earlier story that I wasn't with you."

"Come on. I'm begging you," I said. "Premeditated murder. I may be looking at life in prison, or even worse, death. And you have the power to save me by just telling the truth."

Tom rested his chin on the palm of his hand. "I need to come up with a way to get you off," he said, looking off in the distance. "But at the same time, be sure not to implicate Mr. Wesley in any way. I promised to protect him too. And for my own sake, I have to do that."

Tom and I anguished over that quandary for about ten minutes before I suggested, "What if you just testified that you were with me in the office until 8:20 and you drove me home. You don't have to say a word about Mr. Wesley and that would restore my alibi."

"But they'll hammer me about why I changed my story from what I told the police," Tom said with a grimace. "You know, that you left at 5:30."

"Don't worry about that. We'll come up with something that has nothing to do with Mr. Wesley. But, I need to know whether you'll testify that you were with me up until about nine o'clock." Tom rubbed his face struggling to determine his next move. "Please!"

"Okay, but I'm not saying anything about Mr. Wesley. Nothing. Nothing about his business practices. And absolutely nothing about his phone calls to me. Got it?"

"Yes."

"Another condition," Tom said. "You can't try to implicate Mr. Wesley as a defense argument. You can't even imply it. You got that? Never."

"Okay, I promise we won't."

"It would be suicide if I got Mr. Wesley into any trouble," Tom mumbled as I raced over to shake his hand wildly and thank him profusely.

When I awoke the next day, I knew it was going to be the most important day of my life. I was going to testify first, followed by Tom. Amazingly, I was far more nervous about Tom's testimony than mine. After early morning coaching from Sam, I had complete confidence on the stand. I believe that I told my story with credibility and composure. I said that I knew someone was in my house that night because of my phone calls home. The only real challenge that I faced from cross-examination was to explain how someone could enter my house that night without any signs of break-in. Sam had prepared me for that question and I answered calmly, "I wouldn't know. I was at my office."

When Tom then took the stand, I looked at Mr. Wesley, who shifted in his chair and gazed menacingly at Tom. I turned back around and clasped my fingers together as they rested on the table. I said a quick, silent prayer as Tom was sworn in. Sam approached the stand slowly and confidently. "Are you and the defendant friends?"

"No. I'm his boss at work. I like him, but we're not friends. I never see him outside of a work context."

Sam quoted the date that Kirstin was murdered. "Did you work together that day?"

Tom answered the next series of questions perfectly. He spoke calmly and confidently stating that we were working together in the same conference room in an office over twenty-five miles away from the murder scene. Tom said that he dropped me off at the subway station around nine o'clock.

"So if someone accuses the defendant of doing something at his house that night before 9:00, would that be possible?"

"That would be absolutely impossible," Tom said. "He was with me from about 2:00 until 9:00 that day."

Sam nodded before moving on to the phone call home. Tom testified that we made a call to my house on the speakerphone and a stranger answered. Sam introduced into evidence phone records that verified two calls from the vacant office to my house that night. Sam ended strongly with Tom's 100% assurance that we had dialed my home number from the office in the city around 8:20 PM.

Alicia's face turned red as she shifted papers at her table. I'm not sure if it was from embarrassment or anger. I figured the latter.

"Counselor," the judge said, looking at Alicia. "Your witness."

Alicia slowly stood up and walked over to Tom. "A moment ago, you testified that Tom was with you at 9:00 that night, but that's not what you told the police when they questioned you the day after the crime. Was it?"

"No, it wasn't."

"According to police records, you said that the defendant left the office around 5:30 and you never saw him after that. Isn't that right?"

"That's what I told the police, yes."

"Well, it sounds like you're giving two different stories," Alicia said, throwing her hands up in the air. "One is obviously a lie. Which is it Mr. Brisen?"

"What I told the police was a lie."

Alicia snickered as she turned to look at the jury. "Now why, Mr. Brisen, would you lie to the police during a murder investigation?"

Tom shrugged his shoulders. "It's really silly, but I told my wife that I was working alone that night and I wanted the story to the police to be consistent. I had no idea of the ramifications of this little untruth."

"Wait a minute. Why did you lie to your wife about working alone that night?"

"She wanted me home that night, but I really needed to be in the office. If she had found out that I was working with Mark, she would have insisted that I just delegate it to him. The only way I could stay late that night and avoid a big argument with my wife was to claim that I was the only one that could work that night."

"Fine. You lied to your wife. Why did you lie to the police in a murder investigation?"

"Like I said," Tom said, remaining composed. "I was just trying to keep a consistent story with what I told my wife. I really had no idea it would be so important to the case."

"But now you do," Alicia said, turning to roll her eyes. "What caused this revelation?"

Tom replied that Sam told him it was important. Sam shot me a quick look. I guessed Tom was smart enough to realize it wouldn't sound too good if he said I came to his house. "When I realized an innocent man's freedom was at stake, I had to come forward."

Alicia walked a few paces closer to Tom, actually putting her hands on the railing in front of the witness chair. It was a clear intimidation tactic. "Do you want to see the defendant convicted of this crime?"

"No, I don't."

"You like the defendant, don't you?"

Tom looked over at me, showing a quick smile. "Yes, I do."

"And you don't want to lose him as an employee, which is what would happen if he were sent off to jail?"

"No, I wouldn't."

Alicia backed away from the railing, turned toward the jury and said with a smirk, "Apparently, you don't mind telling little lies to your wife to get a desired work result." Alicia spun back around and looked at Tom. "Isn't this just another little lie that you're telling the jury to save your friend and co-worker?"

"No, it's not a lie," Tom said, tapping his index finger on the railing. "I wouldn't come to a court of law and lie."

"No, you just lie to the police. No further questions."

I truly believe that Tom's testimony was the turning point of the trial. Tom had withstood cross-examination and I had an alibi. In closing arguments, Alicia lambasted Tom's testimony as a last minute, desperate attempt to invent facts so that I had an alibi while Sam was articulate and persuasive in his closing arguments stressing my prior record, alibi, and deep love for Kirstin.

My patience, faith, and prayers paid off when the jury returned a "not guilty" verdict three days later. I was overjoyed with emotion. In the exhilaration, I noticed the Wesley family. Mr. Wesley glared at me. It was a look of hate. His hands were clenched tightly and his eyes were fixed on me. Mrs. Wesley was whispering something to him, but he was ignoring her. I couldn't see Brian anywhere. He must have already bolted from the courtroom. I turned my attention away from the Wesleys and back on the judge who began thanking the jury for their service.

That night, I spent a very quiet night with my family. Even though I was ecstatic with the verdict, I didn't feel much like celebrating. I had been so worried about my own future that I had yet to truly mourn Kirstin's death. I flashed back to that snow globe and thought, "Finally, it had stopped snowing".

I was very eager to get back to a normal life. And for me, it was important to return to work by the end of that week. By that Friday, I was back on the subway heading into my first day at work since Kirstin's death. It felt cathartic to get back to a normal routine.

However, the rollercoaster which my life had become, took another violent turn when I checked my voicemail. The voicemail was from the managing partner in the office. "I'm so sorry to give you this news, but, last night, Tom Brisen, a tax partner who has been with the firm for over fifteen years, was killed in a car crash." I dropped the phone in shock. It felt like someone had ripped out my heart, again!

All I could think was "this was Mr. Wesley's doing." My initial suspicions were heightened when I later found out that only one car was involved. Tom's car had gone off the edge of a cliff just off a winding road. I knew this was no accident. Tom was an extremely safe driver. And he had ridden on that road before. This was payback for testifying for me. Tom had warned me that Mr. Wesley would have him killed. And he did.

With this realization, I spiraled into deep depression, anger, and fear. However, unlike with Kirstin's death, I experienced another emotion as well: guilt. My initial reaction to all of these feelings was to curl up in a ball and shut myself from the rest of the world. And I did, for one long week. I didn't return phone calls and rarely left my house. During that week, showers and shaving were a rarity. I even contemplated suicide. However, the more I thought about it, the angrier I felt, and the more I wanted to take down Mr. Wesley. I knew what I had to do.

I doubted he would have done the actual murder himself. He would have hired a hit man for both Kirstin and Tom. Since my firm handled all financial and tax matters for the Wesley family, I had access to all of their accounts. Many of their brokers already knew me, and it would be customary to ask for detail about transactions running through their accounts. Over the next three weeks, I made numerous phone calls and reviewed a myriad of reports, looking for large withdrawals in any of Mr. Wesley's accounts. I had yet to find a suspicious withdrawal. Still, I knew I would with persistence and creativity. Just as Tom used to tell me, there's always a solution, you just have to know where to look. As I packed up to leave the office that night, I was determined. I was going to get Mr. Wesley.

I got home late that night. Mentally and physically tired, I slowly got out of my car and walked to the curb to check my mail. I could hear music coming from Chris' house from the curb. In an instant, I felt a sack-like bag being thrust over my head and I was suddenly in complete darkness. I struggled, but to no avail because I felt two sets of strong arms holding me in place. I then heard a car pull up and a door being opened. I was quickly shoved into what felt like the back seat. The car then began to move. I felt like screaming, but I knew that would do me no good.

I lay on my side in the back seat with some kind of twine binding my wrists behind my back. I felt a rather strong hand pressing down on my exposed right shoulder to ensure that I did not move. My shoulder, arms, and back all quickly became sore in this uncomfortable position. My mind flashed to Tom, making me swallow hard. My body was filled with a sharp sense of fear that Mr. Wesley was behind this. I could be joining Kirstin and Tom. After about twenty minutes, the car came to a stop and I heard doors being opened. I was taken out of the car and led down what felt like a rocky, dirt path. I remember climbing a few steps into what I believed was some kind of structure. Finally, I was pushed down, falling awkwardly onto a hard wooden chair.

My aching arms were untangled behind my back and refastened tightly in front of me which was much more comfortable. Then, still in a seated position, a rope was wrapped around both of my ankles. Sweat poured down my face from the heat under the bag and from sheer fright. Finally, the bag was lifted. My eyes adjusted to the dim light in what looked like a one-room shack. There was no other furniture in this old rundown hut. There were two men in front of me, neither of whom I recognized. One was short and burly and one was tall and very muscular.

Then, someone from behind slapped the back of my head. "You're a real fool. You know that." My eyes widened. I recognized the voice. It was Brian's. My belief was confirmed as Brian walked in front of me.

Although I was relieved not to see Mr. Wesley, I was still fearful of Brian, who could be a loose cannon. "Brian? What are you doing? Would you please untie me?"

"Uh, I don't think so. You murdered Kirstin and then you start nosing into my family's finances."

"I didn't kill your sister. I swear!"

"Yeah, yeah. Just because a bunch of losers on the jury believed you, don't expect me to." Brian paused to light a cigarette.

"Look Brian," I said, hoping I could talk my way out of this. "I know we don't see eye to eye on much, but there's one thing that we've always had in common."

"What's that?" Brian asked, blowing cigarette smoke in my direction.

"We both loved Kirstin. Granted, we never liked each other, but we had one thing that bonds us together. And that's Kirstin."

"Well, that's where you're wrong," Brian said with a smug look on his face. "I used to love her. You know, she used to follow me around like a little puppy. Did everything I told her. I mean, she idolized me, her big brother." As Brian talked, he gazed off in the distance with a smile on his face. Then, a disgusted look crossed his face as he turned toward me. "Then, she met you. Once you came along, she became completely different. Just a couple of weeks before her death, she threatened me." Brian turned around and surveyed the room. "Can you believe that? Kirstin threatened me."

"Look, no matter how you felt about Kirstin," I said, still hoping to gain Brian as an ally against Mr. Wesley. "I know you didn't want her dead." I took a deep breath. "I know who killed Kirstin."

Brian's eyes widened as he held his cigarette down near his side. "Who did it?" It was a good sign that I had gotten Brian's attention, but I was worried about his reaction to my answer to his question.

I looked at Brian's two henchmen who each had their arms folded in front of them and guns strapped around their waists. "Your father."

"My father!" Brian exclaimed, breaking into laughter. Brian even slapped the short, burly guy on the shoulder as he slowly recovered from his laughter. I was puzzled. I expected anger, not laughter. "Dear old dad, eh." Brian quickly turned serious. "Tell me. Why do you suspect him?"

"Before Tom was murdered, your father admitted to murdering her."

"Really," Brian said, turning to smirk at the short, burly man.

"I was looking into all of your father's accounts because I believe that he ordered a professional hit on Kirstin." Brian's only reaction to my comment was a slight raise of the eyebrows. I wondered if I triggered something in his mind. I continued, "But I haven't found any suspicious, large withdrawals, not yet."

"Enough of the Sherlock Holmes bit," Brian said, throwing his cigarette down on the ground before stepping on it. "You stuck your nose into my family's business," Brian said, pulling out a gun. A shot of fear ran through my body. "I should kill you right now." I swallowed hard as I seemed paralyzed to speak as I stared at the barrel of the gun. "But, I won't," Brian said, pointing the gun toward the ground. I immediately exhaled and allowed my tensed body to relax some. "But, only because another murder so soon after Kirstin and Tom's is just too risky."

"Thank you."

"Don't thank me. Instead of killing you," Brian said, snapping his fingers. As if on cue, the tall muscular guy stepped forward handing Brian a photograph. Brian slowly turned it around. My jaw dropped and my heart rate soared. It was a picture of my parents!

"You so much as look in the direction of my family or its financial records, so help me God, your parents, both of them, are going to have an accident. A serious acci…"

"I understand. I'll drop it, I swear."

"You leave my family alone. I'll leave yours alone."

"I promise I won't do anything more." Then, speaking on emotion, I said, "But, I'd encourage you to get your own proof and go after your father. He masterminded the death of your sister, your innocent sister. You have to stop being a foot soldier for your dad."

"Foot soldier for my dad?" I quickly regretted my last comment. "My dad's the mastermind?" Brian paced the floor a few times like a caged animal. Finally, he gestured to the smaller, burly man and said to me, "This is Joey. Tell him exactly what Tom told you my father said."

"Well," I said, looking up as I tried to think. "Tom said that Mr. Wesley admitted murdering Kirstin. He planned it all…"

"Stop!" Brian said, holding his hand up. He turned to Joey. "Repeat it back, as him." Joey's eyebrows raised a bit at the request. "Do it!"

Joey nodded and said, "Tom said that Mr. Wesley admitted murdering Kirstin. He planned it all."

My jaw dropped and my eyes widened. It wasn't what Joey said that floored me. It was the sound, the voice inflection and the tone. Joey's voice sounded exactly like mine. My mind was racing as I surveyed the room.

"You were in my house," I said to Joey.

"My Lord, he's finally putting the pieces in place. It sure took you long enough."

"You?" I said to Brian with a bewildered look.

Brian turned back toward me and nodded. "Yeah, that's right. I'm the mastermind. Kirstin threatened me once too often. She said she'd go to the police about some things I've done in the family business if I ever interfered in your happiness once you two got married. She was going to hold that over my head for the rest of my life." Brian shook his head and then smirked evilly. "So I had to do something about it."

"But, but it couldn't be you. Mr. Wesley called Tom and admitted to killing Kirstin."

"Haven't you learned anything yet?" Brian asked, slapping me on the side of the head. "It's like that old saying: You can't believe everything you hear." I looked at Brian, still confused. He sighed in disappointment. "If you think Joey does a good impersonation of you, you should hear him do my father." Brian motioned toward Joey who loosened a few of the ropes so I would be able to slowly work my way out. Then, the three men exited, leaving me with the solution to a mystery that I would never be able to tell.

Elevator to Nowhere

"Sorry to keep you folks waiting," the white haired security guard said to the group of three waiting outside the five-story building. It was a few minutes after seven in the morning, an unconscionable time to be waiting outside for the elderly security guard to unlock the building's door. A brisk wind made the wait even more unpleasant. The security guard, who displayed the nametag "Rusty", smiled awkwardly at the irritated trio. As he smiled, a prominently displayed gold tooth seemed to sparkle.

"The building doesn't normally open to the public until eight o'clock," Rusty said as he dug into his pocket for the building keys. "But you three must have one of those special, early morning appointments."

Rusty shifted his coffee mug to his left hand as he unlocked the door. The pleasant warmth of the building encompassed the three as they quickly entered. Rusty put his coffee mug down on a table in the lobby and pulled out a clipboard, announcing, "Everyone needs to sign in. Put your name, who you're visiting, and the time." The middle-aged man quickly signed in, followed by a young man and a middle-aged woman.

"Perfect," Rusty said, admiring the clipboard. "Adam, you're visiting Dr. Van Shoran," Rusty said, looking at the middle-aged man. "And Brett," Rusty said, turning to the young man. "You're visiting Dr. Downs. They're both on the fifth floor."

Rusty turned to the woman. "Maria, Dr. Jamison is on the fourth floor. You all can take the elevator right here." The elevator door opened and a light flashed, indicating that the elevator was heading up.

Adam held the elevator door with his left hand and, with a smile, waved Maria and Brett in. Maria dipped her head slightly to show her appreciation as she entered. Maria and Brett hit the floor buttons and the elevator doors shut.

Adam looked at his reflection in the small mirror around the elevator floor buttons. He adjusted his tie slightly and pushed his gold glasses higher up the bridge of his nose. His well-tailored blue suit perfectly fit his lanky body.

Brett, carrying a backpack over his right shoulder, stood almost six feet tall. He had a sturdy build and wavy, blond hair. Lacking a good night's sleep, he yawned heavily as he stood in the back corner of the elevator. He slouched a bit as he leaned against the side wall.

Maria, the shortest of the three, had black hair, which draped down to her shoulders in back. She carried an elegant black purse over her right shoulder. She seemed to convey a quiet, but confident posture as she stood on the opposite side of the elevator from the two men.

The three stood, silently, looking up at the digital display. They could feel the elevator rising as the display changed to the second floor, and then the third floor. Maria moved a step closer to the elevator door as she eyed the display. The three on the display disappeared and was replaced with darkness. The elevator seemed to pause, bob up and down a bit, before coming to a halt.

But, the doors didn't open. Three sets of eyes looked at the now blank digital display and then back to the doors. As seconds passed by, it appeared to all that the elevator was stuck.

"Ah man," Brett said.

Adam was the first to act, stepping forward to press the red button marked "help".

"This is building security. Is there a problem?" a voice responded through elevator's speaker. It was clear to everyone that the voice was Rusty's.

"Yeah," Adam said. "The elevator's stuck."

"Oh my gosh," Rusty said, not inspiring confidence from anyone in the elevator. "Well, I'll have it back up and running in no time. Just hold on."

Maria sighed heavily and Brett slumped back to rest on the small railing that ran across the back wall of the elevator. Adam glanced at his watch before folding his arms in front of his chest. Adam's eyes widened at what happened next. The previously lit #4 and #5 buttons went dark.

Adam hit the red help button again and said, "Hey, all of the buttons went dark. What's going on?"

"Don't be alarmed," Rusty said. "Give me a few minutes. I'll get back to you soon."

"Aw great," Brett said, as he sat down on the floor, resting his head against the side wall.

"Well, seeing how we're going to be together for a while, let me introduce myself," Maria said. She introduced herself, and Adam and Brett followed suit. "I'm here to see my psycho-therapist. What kind of doctors are you guys seeing?"

"I'm seeing a psycho-therapist too," Adam replied.

Adam and Maria both turned to look at Brett. "Same with me, but I think the technical term is a shrink," Brett said. "Or what I like to call, a big waste of time."

"Waste of time?" Maria asked perplexed. "You're an adult. If you feel that way, why do you even go?"

Brett smiled for a moment as he contemplated whether he'd answer Maria's question. "It's court mandated that I see a therapist. It's part of my plea bargain. Today's my first session with Dr. Downs." Adam raised his eyebrows and Maria nervously bobbed her head up and down. "The court thinks I have an anger problem. So, now that I've spilled my guts, what about you two?"

"Well, I'm here for marriage therapy. But, it's a big joke," Adam said. "Explain this to me. How's some stranger going to tell me how to work things out with my wife? And here's the weirdest thing. My therapist, Dr. Van Shoran, wants to see just me."

"I thought marriage counseling was conducted with both partners present," Maria said as she rubbed her chin.

"Exactly my point." Adam sighed before saying, "My wife's therapist recommended him, so he's supposed to be good. But, since this is my first visit, I don't know anything about him."

"Well, you know one thing," Brett said. "His methods are a little unorthodox." Brett turned and looked at Maria. "So what are you seeing your therapist for?"

"Depression."

"So, is your therapist any good?" Adam asked.

"Dr. Jamison?" Maria said before shrugging her shoulders. "Well, he's a good listener."

Adam laughed. "Oh wow, these therapists have a pretty good gig, don't they? They got two new customers who don't want to be here, and one returning who gets the same service a wall could provide." The other two chuckled at Adam's remark, momentarily forgetting that they were trapped in the elevator.

Growing tired of standing, Maria joined Brett, sitting on the elevator floor. Adam took off his suit jacket and draped it over a railing in the elevator. He looked at his watch and shook his head with displeasure. "I got this early morning appointment so I could get to work before the market opens," Adam said, taking a seat. "Who knows if I'll make it now?"

"Have you guys seen a therapist before?" Maria asked.

"My wife and I used to see a marriage therapist together," Adam said. "It was useless. Even the therapist realized he wasn't doing any good. He ended up referring me to Dr. Van Shoran."

"How about you?" Maria asked Brett.

"No, but I know it's going to be a waste of time. Some guy judging me by what he's read in some book. Going off, telling me acting on my rage is bad."

"Hey," Adam said. "I couldn't agree with you more about a therapist telling you psycho-babble. But the anger thing, you do have to get that under control."

"What do you know about anger? Sometimes, it's best to get it out. It's not good to keep it bottled up."

"I know a lot about anger," Adam said. "Do you want to know why I'm here?"

"You told us," Brett said, rolling his eyes. "Your marriage is in trouble."

"Yeah, but why is my marriage in trouble? It's in trouble because in a moment of rage, I slapped my wife."

"My gosh," Maria said, covering her mouth.

"Oh please," Brett said. "Let's not get dramatic. It's just a slap. I'm sure she wasn't physically hurt from a slap."

"You don't get it," Adam said. "It's not the physical damage that's relevant. It's the mental. She's had many emotions toward me during our rocky marriage: anger, frustration, disappointment, but never fear. Now, she has fear." Adam paused as he closed his eyes. He slowly shook his head before opening his eyes again. "Trust me. There is no worse emotion that someone you love can have toward you. She looks at me different now and it's the source of all of our problems."

"You're still young," Maria said to Brett. "But you'll learn in life you are judged by your actions. Therefore, you always need to have control of them."

There was an awkward silence. Brett felt a little uncomfortable receiving advice from two strangers and wanted to divert the conversation away from him. "Say, you said you're seeing a therapist about depression. What are you so depressed about?" Brett asked Maria.

"My husband died in a car accident a year ago." Brett and Adam dipped their heads in mourning. "We have two young children and sometimes, I just feel like I can't go on." Maria reached in her purse to grab a tissue. She wiped the corner of her eyes.

"Sorry to hear that," Brett mumbled, regretting his probing question.

"As I see it, you two are lucky," Maria said.

"Why?" Brett said. "What are you talking about?"

"Well, you're a young guy with his whole life ahead of him. All you have to do is learn to keep your emotions in check. I mean, that's completely in your power." Brett stared at the floor as Maria turned toward Adam. "And you have a spouse who is alive. You have the power to save your marriage."

"No, not necessarily. If my wife decides she wants to end the marriage, there isn't a thing I can do." Adam made a circle with his hand. "Zilch! For all I know, she may have already made up her mind."

"But, she hasn't," Maria said.

"How would you know?"

"Because you said that she wanted to do marriage therapy. That means that she still wants to try to make it work. And frankly, I don't understand why you wouldn't embrace therapy 100%."

"I'm here, aren't I?" Adam said, holding both arms away from his body.

"Yes, you are," Maria said nodding. "But, you told Brett earlier that you thought this marriage therapy was a big joke. I would spend 24 hours a day in a therapist's office if it could bring back my husband."

"It's been over fifteen minutes. I'm going to miss the market's opening," Adam said, getting up and pressing the help button. They waited for Rusty's familiar voice, but there was no response. Adam pressed it again and yelled into the speaker, "We need help! We're stuck in the elevator! We're stuck in the elevator!" Again, there was no response. Adam began pressing the help button again.

"Might as well save your energy," Brett said. "It doesn't appear that anyone's listening."

"Where could Rusty be?" Maria asked.

"Who knows!" Adam said, throwing his hands up before taking his seat back on the floor.

"I have a question for you two," Maria said. "Do you believe that everything happens for a reason?"

"What? Like getting trapped in this elevator?" Brett asked with a wrinkled forehead. "Nah, sometimes, stuff just happens."

"What about you?" Maria asked Adam.

"I don't know," Adam said with a shoulder shrug. "As annoying as it is being trapped in an elevator, I'm enjoying talking to you two. I've learned a few things too. So, maybe it was meant to be."

"I have a question then," Maria said, capturing Adam and Brett's complete attention. "If everything happens for a reason, why did my husband have to die leaving behind me and two young kids?" There was silence in the elevator. "Why?"

Adam looked down at the floor unable to answer while Brett said, "I don't know."

"You know the last thing I ever told my husband, the love of my life, before he died?" Maria asked.

"What?"

"Damn you. That's what I told my husband. He was working late and said he couldn't make it home for a special dinner I planned. I said 'damn you' and hung up. He died in a car accident that night, rushing to get home." Adam dipped his head and looked vacantly at the floor. Brett stared right at Maria, waiting for her to speak again. "Do you know why I said that to him?" Maria asked, looking at Brett.

"No. Why?"

"Because I was angry. I couldn't control my emotions." Brett grimaced, as it appeared that Maria's comments hit home. "And because of that, my husband's dead."

"You didn't kill your husband," Adam said sternly.

"If I didn't make him rush home, he wouldn't have crashed."

"Adam's right," Brett said. "You did not cause your husband's death. Like I said before, sometimes stuff just happens."

The three continued to sit down on the elevator floor, patiently waiting for the elevator to move again. Maria, who once again had to reach into her purse for tissues to wipe her eyes, was beginning to regain her composure. "Well Brett," Maria said before taking a deep breath. "Adam and I disclosed the circumstances why we're here. What did you do that caused the judge to order you to seek therapy?"

Brett, who was slouching, sat up so that his lower back touched the wall. He crossed his legs and clasped his hands together before saying, "I was driving down the street and this punk cuts me off. I mean, he almost ran me off the road. I honk at him and he gives me the finger. And I just lost it."

"What happened?" Adam asked.

"I caught up to him and forced him off the road. I beat him up real bad." Adam and Maria stared at Brett in shock. Feeling the burning of their eyes, Brett said, "I know it's bad, alright."

"It's not just bad," Adam said. "It's stupid. He could have had a gun."

"Hey! Nobody gives me the finger and gets away with it."

"The finger?" Adam said in disbelief. "Who cares? You could have been killed."

"Well, sometimes I feel like death's not such a bad thing," Brett said as he looked at the floor.

"What?" Maria said. "What are you talking about?"

"I've contemplated suicide," Brett said as he looked back up. "When bad things happen like getting thrown in jail, I wonder whether my life's really worth living."

"You're young. I've been there," Adam said. "But, trust me. Getting upset because someone raises his middle finger is stupid. I mean, it's an additional finger away from getting the peace sign. Who cares?!"

"I'm not stupid. Looking back, I realize I shouldn't have done it, but I just get caught up in the moment."

"Well, I guess therapy would help you deal with that," Maria said, causing Brett to nod slightly.

"Ah jeez," Adam said, looking at his watch. "It's been over a half hour." He got up and hit the red help button again. "I have to get into the office before the market opens today."

"You keep saying that," Brett said. "Why? Why is it so important that you get to the office when the market opens?"

Adam turned and walked a few steps to a sitting Brett. Adam put both hands on his knees, bending down to come eye to eye with Brett. "It's important because if I'm not there, someone else at the firm will have to put all my orders in."

"So? Someone else puts your orders in. What's the big deal?"

"They might not do it right," Adam said, gritting his teeth. "I'm the best broker in the business. My clients know that and expect only the best."

"Are you a better broker or a husband?" Maria interjected.

Adam spun around to look at Maria. "What kind of question is that?"

"An honest one. Let me ask a different question. Do you care more about your job or your marriage?"

"My marriage, of course," Adam said, putting his hands on his hips.

"I see," Maria said. "I guess then it is only logical that you spend more time thinking, worrying, and troubleshooting aspects of your marriage than aspects of your job."

"You're beginning to sound like a therapist," Adam said, taking his seat.

"I'm not a therapist, but I was married to a man who was consumed by his job."

For the first time since the three were in the elevator, a prolonged silence occurred. It's as if each one of them wanted to stop and mull over their earlier conversations. "Hear that?" Brett said excitedly.

"Hear what?" Maria asked.

"Near this wall," Brett said, pressing his ear up against the elevator wall. "I hear another elevator moving. The problem has been fixed."

Adam's forehead wrinkled. "Why isn't this elevator moving?"

Brett pulled his ear away from the wall. "Something's not right."

"I'm calling Rusty," Maria said, starting to rise.

"No, let me," Adam said, stopping Maria from getting up. He walked over to the speaker and pressed the help button again, but with no response. "Is there anyone there? We're stuck in the elevator!" Still, no response. "I don't like this." Brett slowly rose, joining a standing Adam. "The way I see it, there are only two possibilities that could explain what's going on," Adam said.

"What's that?" Maria asked as she joined the men on her feet.

"Either something is mechanically wrong with this elevator, and security has no clue how to fix it, or..."

"Do you think we could survive if this elevator plummets four floors?" Brett asked.

"Don't even talk about stuff like that," Maria said with disgust.

"Or, the second possibility," Adam said, trying to regain the attention. "This elevator is fine. Someone is keeping us locked in here on purpose."

"What?" Maria said squinting. "That's crazy."

"Is it?" Adam asked as he tilted his head. "Answer me this. Why isn't Rusty even responding to our help calls?"

"Someone wants us dead," Brett said.

"Dead?" Adam said with a look of disbelief. "What are you talking about? I'm just suggesting that someone wants us detained."

"Detained? Why?" Brett asked. "Why would anyone want to lock the three of us up in an elevator? There's no reason for it." Brett looked over at the unlit elevator buttons and dark display. "But, knocking us off, that's plausible."

"Are you crazy?" Adam said. "No one wants to kill us."

"Some people would love to see me dead," Brett said. "Like the father of the kid I beat up, for example."

"What's that got to do with us?" Adam asked with both hands on his hips.

"You two, are what the military calls, collateral damages," Brett said in a serious tone.

"What's with this fixation about death?" Maria asked.

"I don't have a fixation about death. I just don't want to die, alright. I don't want to die!"

Maria and Adam exchanged glances, shocked by Brett's outburst. "You told us earlier that you think about suicide a lot," Maria said. "Now, you're shouting that you don't want to die. What's going on?"

"I don't know. I think it's a control thing."

"I don't understand," Maria said to Brett.

"When I contemplate suicide, I'm taking a decisive action. I'm taking control of the situation. Here, I have no control, and it's driving me nuts."

"I don't buy it," Adam said. "Control has nothing to do with it. If you don't want to be killed, it means you don't want to die. And if you don't want to die, you can't want to commit suicide."

"I think this goes back to controlling your emotions," Maria said. "Just because you feel a certain way, you don't have to act upon it. If you feel mad, you can't beat people up. And if you feel sad, you can't want to commit suicide."

"I have good news!" Rusty's voice said through the speaker. Maria, Adam, and Brett all jumped up with the sound of his voice. "We've solved the problem. The elevator should be moving any moment."

The fourth and fifth floor buttons relit and the elevator slowly moved up for a bit, and finally, the doors opened. "Elevator is working fine now," Rusty said over the speaker. "Those going to the fifth floor should remain on the elevator."

"It was really nice to meet both of you," Maria said, stepping off the elevator. As the doors closed, Maria shouted as she waved, "Wish you guys the best with everything."

"Well," Brett said, turning to Adam as the elevator began to rise again. "I'm going to miss her."

Adam's lips remained tight as he nodded his head before saying, "Me too." The elevator bell dinged and the doors opened again. "I believe this is our stop," Adam said, holding the door open.

Brett turned to pick up his backpack and noticed a black purse. "Maria left her purse."

Still holding the elevator doors, Adam motioned with his free hand. "Bring it. After I check in with Dr. Van Shoran, I'll drop it off with Maria at Dr. Jamison's office."

Brett shrugged his shoulders, picked up the purse, and handed it to Adam. And at long last, Adam and Brett left the elevator. The wall opposite the elevator displayed the location of the doctor offices on the floor. The sign showed Dr. Downs, with an arrow to the right, Suite 510. One line lower read Dr. Van Shoran, with an arrow to the right, Suite 510.

"It looks like our doctors share the same office," Brett said, pointing to the wall.

"Well, apparently, our adventure together continues," Adam said before they headed down the hallway and into Suite 510.

"I had an appointment at seven o'clock with Dr. Van Shoran," Adam said to the receptionist. The receptionist was an older, white haired lady who wore small glasses on the edge of her nose.

"I had an appointment at the same time with Dr. Downs," Brett said.

"Seven o'clock?" the receptionist said. "You're both fifty minutes late."

"Actually," Brett said, gritting his teeth. "We were on time. We got here at seven, but have been stuck in the building's elevator for the last fifty minutes."

The receptionist offered a fake smile before saying, "Regardless of the reason, you're fifty minutes late, and your appointments have been cancelled."

"Then, when can I reschedule?" Adam asked, putting his hands on the receptionist's desk.

"You can't," the receptionist replied, shaking her head. "Neither of you can."

"What?!" Brett exclaimed. "Why not?"

"If you're more than thirty minutes late for an appointment, you're dropped as a client," the receptionist said. "It's Dr. Van Shoran's and Dr. Downs' policy. They have busy schedules."

"This is ridiculous. It's not our fault!"

"Calm down Brett," Adam said, stepping in between him and the receptionist's desk.

"We can give you referrals to several other licensed therapists," the receptionist said. She reached into a drawer and handed Adam two cards.

Adam grabbed the cards and pushed Brett back toward the door. As they exited, Adam said, "Let's at least give Maria her purse back." They found the stairwell to the fourth floor and walked into Dr. Jamison's office.

Dr. Jamison's receptionist was a young man in his mid twenties. "We're looking for a Maria, she's a patient." Adam, noticing the empty waiting room, said, "She must be with Dr. Jamison now."

"Dr. Jamison is not with a patient named Maria," the receptionist responded. He grabbed a hold of the mouse and began clicking it as he looked at the computer screen. "No, no one named Maria. Why are you two asking?"

"We have her purse," Adam said, lifting the purse. "She inadvertently left it in the elevator."

"It's possible Maria is just a nickname. Proper names are always used for appointments," the receptionist said. "But I can't give out patient information without you at least giving me her last name."

Adam paused to look over to Brett. "Do you remember Maria's last name?"

"No," Brett said, shaking his head.

"Well, I'm sorry, with just a first name, there's nothing more I can help you with."

"You know what," Adam said, turning toward Brett. "She put her last name down on the sign-in sheet. So Rusty would know." Adam turned back toward the receptionist. "Could I call down to security on the first floor?"

The receptionist nodded. "I'll dial them for you." After a couple of moments, he handed Adam the phone.

"Hello, security desk," a voice said over the phone. Adam realized it was not Rusty's voice.

"Hi, I'm looking for Rusty. Can you put him on the phone?"

"Rusty? Did you mean to dial the security desk on the first floor?"

"Yes. I'm looking for Rusty. He's a security guard. Older guy, wavy, white hair, gold tooth."

"You must be mistaken sir. There's no one that works in security that fits that description. And there definitely is no one named Rusty."

Adam's forehead wrinkled as he slowly handed the phone back to the receptionist.

"What did they say?" Brett asked.

"They said that no one named Rusty works with security."

"That's crazy," Brett said.

"It gets worse," Adam said. "They said no one works there fitting his description. Older, wavy white hair, gold tooth."

"Hmm," the receptionist said. "If I didn't know any better, I'd think you were talking about Dr. Downs."

"What?" Adam said, turning toward the receptionist.

"Your description of the security guard. It sounds like a description of Dr. Downs. He's a doctor on the fifth floor."

"He's the doctor I had my appointment with," Brett said. "None of this is making any sense. Why would Dr. Downs pose as a security guard?"

"I don't know, but we have to get in contact with Maria. Maybe, the three of us can confront Dr. Downs about this."

"Hey!" Brett said, snapping his fingers. "Check her purse. Maria had to have some ID. Maybe even some business cards so we can contact her."

"Good idea." Adam rummaged through the purse, pulling out a pocketbook. He opened it up. His eyes bulged out and his jaw dropped in shock. It was as if Adam had seen a ghost.

"What's the matter?" Brett asked.

"I found Maria's ID, but it doesn't say Maria."

"What does it say?"

Adam held up the card. "It says Dr. Deborah Van Shoran."

Murder in a Country Town

I peered through the top of my rifle as I held it in a tight grip. My hands were steady and my concentration was strong. Devoid of perspiration, I felt cool, calm and collected as my mind focused on the upcoming kill. I hunched below the high, brown weeds as I looked up at the darkening sky. There was a rustle in a bush in the distance before a duck took flight. I quickly adjusted my aim and fired.

"Bang!" the rifle roared. A split second later the duck plummeted to the ground. "In just one shot," I said to myself as I raised my eyebrows and slightly nodded my head. I crouched back down in the high weeds.

As I waited, I admired the picturesque landscape and inhaled the cool, crisp air. Being wealthy, successful and modestly famous has its perks. It has allowed me the wherewithal to get away from it all.

The peaceful surroundings were a perfect backdrop to this hunting trip. I loved to spend time in the country, which was devoid of the hustle and bustle of city life. I admired the sheer beauty of nature as I looked over at the pond in the distance. This was the site where the most daring and brilliant idea was born, the idea to kill Sheriff Brian Parsons.

I had to admit that part of me, a large part, really liked him. The pride of the small country town of Rossmore, Sheriff Parsons had an endearing arrogance to him which befit the tough talking lawman. He was quite a character. Sharp as a tack, he worked tirelessly and often heroically to get to the truth. Everybody liked him. I think people admired his work ethic and his ideals. He had quickly become a local icon and had long ago become better known than me.

Sheriff Parsons had a thin mustache and short, black hair. With a military background, he believed in rules, order and the chain of command. In private, he would sit for hours with a furrowed brow and wrinkled forehead trying to put the pieces together to solve yet another crime. In contrast, in public, he acted quickly and impulsively. But the thing that moved the fastest on his body was always his mouth. "Think you can get away with murder. Not in my town! Not on my watch!" he would loudly boast. And he was always right. He always caught his man, or woman, as the case may be.

An evil smile curled my lips as I hunched deep in the weeds waiting for the next duck to take flight. This would be one murder that Sheriff Parsons would never solve… *his*.

I know what you're thinking. "Why would anyone want to kill the good ol' sheriff?" Clearly, every murder has to have a motive. Well, how's this? One of the many characters that he has put in jail over the years, gets out looking for some payback. Or maybe a crooked, ambitious deputy sees the sheriff as an obstacle to running the town. So you see, there are many motives out there.

The more important question is, "Why would *I* want to kill him? The easy answer is jealousy, but there's more to it than that. I've grown tired of him. I just think it's time for a change in the town of Rossmore. And I have to admit, I'd enjoy reading all of the publicity that his death would surely bring.

It's not like I woke up one day and decided that I had to knock off the good ol' Sheriff Parsons. I have been plotting this out for over two months, weighing the pros and the cons, until today when I finally made my decision. I knew I had to make him a dead man, before I changed my mind.

The key question was how. Another evil smile curled across my face as I looked down at my rifle. How about a gunshot to the head while he was sleeping? That would be perfect. I decided I would write-off the sheriff tonight.

That night, with rifle still in hand, I slowly walked in darkness up the stairs. Once I reached the top of the stairs, I could hear snoring from the bedroom. I quietly and carefully tiptoed over to a room, which was a makeshift study and sat down at the desk. "Maybe he should have a suicide note. That'll cross up the authorities," I thought to myself as I rubbed my face. I turned on the computer as I could still faintly hear the snoring from the adjacent bedroom. I reminded myself that I had to be as quiet as possible.

Then, a strange thing happened. For some reason, my composure quickly evaporated. My heart began to race and my hands shook slightly as Microsoft Word loaded on the computer. I took a deep breath and exhaled audibly. I buried my face in my hands for a moment to garner the strength to do the previously unthinkable. There was no turning back now. I had made my decision. I slowly removed my hands from my face and moved them over the keyboard and began to type the letters. I didn't look at the screen as I typed. Instead, I focused on my fingers, which were pounding with renewed vigor on the keyboard. As I typed, I began to feel empowered. With each letter, I felt myself becoming bigger and more important than the sheriff. I abruptly stopped and slowly lifted my head to look at the words on the screen.

I pressed my right elbow on the desk and rested my chin in the palm of my right hand. I read the paragraph that I typed.

"When no one answered the doorbell, the deputy broke into the house early that morning, frantically looking for Sheriff Parsons. Serial killer Frank Lanson, who had escaped from jail in the middle of the night, was likely leaving the small country town as quickly as possible. He had to alert the sheriff, the deputy thought as he raced upstairs. The deputy stopped suddenly once he reached the bedroom, seeing Sheriff Parsons' lifeless body, still in pajamas, shot in the head. A gun and a handwritten note rested next to the body. The note read: I couldn't go on knowing that I let Frank escape."

"The media stir will be huge," I said smiling. "Everyone will want to know if Sheriff Parsons really committed suicide. This mystery book will be a best seller for sure." I shut down the computer and joined my snoring wife in bed. Finally, I would escape the shadow of longtime series character Brian Parsons.

The Intuition of Henry Burrows

"That doesn't look real, not even close," Henry Burrows said as he watched Freddie Krueger maul one of his victims. Without a gasp or even a small flinch, Henry watched the horror film as he casually munched on popcorn. Perhaps the movie didn't faze him because of the 30 years he served as chief inspector where he had witnessed all too many real, gruesome murders.

Nothing scared old Henry Burrows any more. A bachelor, Henry was home alone on this night. His body sank deep down in his favorite reclining chair with his feet propped up. He dug his hands into the bowl of hot, buttery popcorn that rested on his lap. Next to the popcorn, a basket of Hershey kisses rested on the table next to him. He reached into the basket and unwrapped the chocolate from its foil before throwing it in his mouth. Popcorn and chocolate was the kind of diet that his doctor had warned him to avoid. But, he wasn't worried. He knew how to take care of himself.

"Don't go over to the window, cuz you know he's out there," Henry said, shaking his head at the television. Henry knew how to size up any situation and he could smell danger a mile away.

Just outside Henry's home on the sidewalk, a blood drenched ax murderer stopped in his tracks. On this dark night, the ax murderer looked up and noticed that Henry's porch light was on. Someone was home. A wicked smile crossed his face.

He had already visited two homes on the block that night. Henry's would be the third. A hideous sight, the ax murderer had several cuts on his face and a deep gash on his right arm that continued to bleed. His hair was a frazzled mess and his shirt was partially ripped near his chest. He slowly began his trek up Henry's driveway.

Inside the house, Henry's eyes remained glued to the television set. He watched without emotion as the young female character got slashed in the throat by Freddie Krueger after he leaped through the window. "Told you to stay away from the window," he said to the television.

Henry scratched his gray hair, wondering whether the movie was really worthy of his time. Just as he completed that thought, the doorbell rang. He muted the television with the remote control and slowly made his way to the front door.

Just outside Henry's home on the doorstep, the ax murderer waited. While he was waiting, he noticed that the door did not have a peephole. He held a big bag in his left hand in which he would stuff any valuables that he would get out of this house. He listened quietly and wondered whether anyone really was home.

But then, the ax murderer heard the footsteps coming toward the door. A sinister smile curled on his lips. The footsteps became louder as they came closer and closer. And then they stopped. There was silence and the only thing he could hear was the faint sound of the wind blowing through nearby trees. The relative silence was then broken by the sound of the front door's bolt lock being released. He lifted his bloody ax in anticipation of the door being opened.

After unbolting the top lock, Henry paused for a moment. He did not know why he paused, but he did. He always had a strong nose for danger, but the only thing he could smell now were the remnants of the buttery popcorn on his fingers.

Henry opened the door and his eyes met the eyes of the ax murderer. Time seemed to freeze. Henry stood speechless.

The ax murderer quickly brought down his right hand, which was holding the ax. He opened his bag and shoved it forward. "Trick or treat!"

"Now that looks real," Henry said, extending the basket of Hershey kisses. "For that costume, take as many as you want, kid."

The Perfect Crime

It was the perfect crime. My dictionary defines perfection as "the highest degree of proficiency, skill, or excellence". And that, at the risk of sounding arrogant, would make me the perfect criminal.

If you ask someone to name the all-time perfect criminal, no matter who they say, they'd be wrong. That's because the perfect criminal is never even suspected of wrongdoing. You see, it's someone you have never heard of. A perfect crime occurs when the entire country knew about a crime, but no one knows who was responsible. Even better, the perfect criminal commits a crime that no one realizes was a crime.

No one thinks of me as a criminal. A former police officer myself, one of my closest friends was none other than the town's sheriff. I'm a highly respected member of the community and I look the part. My appearance is always impeccable because the impression one instills is everything. In addition to staying in shape physically, it's equally important to be on top of my game mentally. My strongest attributes have always been my determination and intelligence. Thinking several steps ahead of everyone else is always critical.

For two years, I have served as head of security at a museum, which now houses one of the country's most valuable diamonds. Donated to the museum through the will of a wealthy, family-less man, the prized diamond was required to remain in the museum for all time. The museum was thrilled with this donation because visitors flocked year round to see this display. As a trusted and skilled member of the community, I was asked to oversee the security system of the prized diamond. Nothing, including a pen from the gift shop, has ever been stolen from the museum under my two-year watch. That was about to change.

To pull off the plan, I needed the help of two accomplices. I knew who I wanted. It was a couple in their late twenties. I've only worked with them twice before, but I knew they would both leap at the opportunity to get their grubby hands on that diamond.

The woman, who went by Jill Andersen, didn't mind taking risks to win the big prize. Jill's black hair drooped over her eyes in front and fell down to the top of her shoulders in back. No matter what the occasion, I don't believe Jill would ever wear jewelry or make-up. A tough little cookie, Jill's smallish frame belied the fact that she was very strong, both in will and pure muscle. She talked tough and made it known that no one would take advantage of her.

Jill's husband, on the other hand, believed in talking softly and carrying a big stick. The "stick" always was either a gun or knife. I called him Johnny, short for Johnny B. Bad. Johnny was a criminal's criminal. In trouble with the law throughout his life, Johnny was always looking for a big score, as he called it. Devoid of morals, he'd steal from an elderly woman, a baby, and a priest if he'd be assured of only one thing- he wouldn't get caught. Unlike his wife, Johnny was always more of a smooth talker than a tough talker. He liked to say Jill's most successful crime was stealing his heart. He had boyish good looks with a muscular torso and long scraggily hair.

I heard a loud knock. I walked toward the front door, but stopped at the mirror in the hallway. I ran a comb through my hair, adjusted my eyeglasses, and dusted some lint off my sweater. I heard another pound at the door before I headed toward it.

I opened the door just as Jill was about to pound it again. "Well," I said, eyeing the young couple. Jill still held her right arm awkwardly in the air. "Why not alert the whole neighborhood of your presence? Not smart."

Jill dropped her right arm to her side. "Wouldn't have happened if you didn't take an hour to open the door."

I stepped over to the side and motioned for the two to come in. The three of us sat around the table and discussed the plan. They had known for over three weeks that they were going to help me steal the diamond, but I had yet to explain exactly how. When we sat down at the table, I knew it was time. I first explained to them that my presence at the museum was rare. I was really hired to design the security system, not monitor it. However, I actually did watch over the security system and staff at the museum once every two weeks. This Friday was one of those days and that was the day we would take the diamond.

"I don't get it," Johnny said. "You want us to steal the diamond when the museum is open. That ain't smart." Johnny tapped the side of his head. "There could be tons of people there. Why not break into the museum in the middle of the night and snatch the diamond then?"

"No," I said. I took off my glasses and rubbed my eyes. "Look, the building has too much security when it's closed. It will be a lot easier when it's open. When the museum is open, there are just two security measures that protect the diamond. Both of these measures can be disarmed by cutting two wires inside a panel in a locked room. We'll call that room the security room." I slid across the table a sheet of paper showing a color diagram of the inside panel. "Cutting the red wire will disconnect the alarm that is set on the diamond's glass case which is mounted inside a museum wall. Cutting the blue wire disconnects all video surveillance equipment."

"What about this green wire?" Johnny asked, tapping on the diagram.

"I was about to get to that. Whatever you do, don't touch the green wire. That's a further precaution I took when setting up the system. If the green wire is cut, it will set off a separate general alarm which will loudly ring throughout the museum."

"Cut the blue and red," Johnny said. "Don't touch the green. Got it."

"Remind me," Jill said. "Why do we even need you to pull this off? Sounds like we're doing all the work."

"Oh you need me," I said, shooting Jill a glare. "As soon as your hubby over there forces that security room door open, it sets off a beeper to the head watchman on duty. And on this day, that's me. When I get that signal, I will immediately evacuate everyone from the room where the diamond is located." I got up from my chair and walked over to Johnny. I put my right hand on his shoulder, coming eye to eye with him. "You have no more than two minutes to enter the security room, break the panel, cut the two wires, and leave the security room."

"Piece a cake old man," Johnny said, holding both arms out away from his body.

When Johnny did this, I could see a gun strap inside his jacket. "Hey, don't bring the gun to the museum, okay?"

"Hey, where I go, my gun goes." Johnny pulled his jacket away from the left side of his chest, revealing not only the gun strap but also the gun.

"No, eventually everyone will be searched. The gun will just raise suspicion."

"Okay," Johnny said. "You win old man. No gun."

I nodded at the resolution as I walked back around the table and sat in my chair. "Hey," Jill said. "You said you were going to evacuate everyone out of the room with the diamond. But if you do that, how am I going to get the diamond?"

"I'll evacuate everyone but you," I said to Jill with a smile. "You will hide in a supplies closet which is normally locked. It won't be that day." Jill nodded. "As soon as I evacuate everyone from the room, you'll break the glass case that holds the diamond with a crowbar."

"What if someone hears her?" Johnny asked.

"That won't happen," I said, shaking my head. "Of course, the alarm will by then be disconnected. And I would have closed the door leading to the room with the diamond in it. I'll be barking out orders. There will be a lot of commotion. No one will hear Jill."

"So I take the diamond and then what?" Jill asked.

"Once you take the diamond, you'll go back into the closet," I said. There's a small window at the top of the closet that leads outside the museum. You'll need to break that window and drop the diamond outside where Johnny will be waiting. He'll take the diamond and hide it in a locked compartment embedded in the walls of a water well about two hundred feet away from the museum building."

"You must have spent a lot of time thinking this one up old man," Johnny said with a chuckle.

"Now this is important," I said, coming eye to eye with Johnny. "Time is of the essence. It's not an easy climb to get to the hiding place. You'll have to do it quickly and get back to the ticketing area of the museum. That's where I'll do a roll call once I determine the diamond is missing. You must be present, okay?"

"Got it," Johnny said.

"I'll call in the police and they'll do a search, but they won't find the diamond. Eventually, everyone will be released. Once things calm down, the three of us will go back to the hiding place and retrieve the diamond."

"I like the plan," Jill said. "It's brilliant"

"It's more than brilliant," I said. "It's perfect."

The doors to the museum were opened promptly Friday morning at 9:00 AM. At about nine forty-five, the museum had about thirty visitors. Johnny waited in the corridor for my signal. We were at what I call "the point of no return". As soon as I signaled to Johnny, our plan would be irreversibly set into action.

I'm usually hit with a pang of nervousness or self doubt at the point of no return; the lingering feeling that I somehow forgot something or the feeling that I somehow miscalculated. But, not this time. I felt completely confident. Strange, because the fact is I was trying to steal one of the country's most prized possessions with only the help of two inexperienced and really unknown kids. Still, I knew this would be the perfect crime, and my personal risk was, as usual, next to zero. I signaled to Johnny.

I continued to "make my rounds", patrolling the museum. A few minutes later, my beeper went off. I waited about a minute before contacting my two security staff on their belt radio. "Barry, my beeper went off. We may have a breach in the security room. Check it out. And Darryl, I don't want to take any chances. Make sure the diamond is secure and then evacuate the diamond room."

Both men acknowledged my order by saying, "I'm on it."

About a minute later, Barry called me back. "Someone ripped apart the security system. The alarm is down."

"Down? I'll be right over." When I got to the security room, Barry was waiting for me. "Oh no," I said, seeing the security panel ripped open. I inspected the panel. "They cut the blue and red wires. The diamond is exposed." I grabbed my radio. "Darryl, where are you?"

"I'm standing guard outside the diamond room. Just like you asked me."

"Is the diamond secure?"

"Yeah, I got a visual before evacuating the room. It's safe."

"I want you to check again," I ordered.

Darryl sighed. "Okay, hang on." Within a few moments he was back on. "I don't believe this, but the diamond is gone."

I immediately had the gates to the museum closed so no one could get in or get out. I asked Darryl to call the police. Barry and I gathered everyone in the museum's ticketing area. The crowd was getting restless as many guests demanded to know what was going on.

"If I could have everyone's attention!" I yelled, standing on top of a bench. It took a moment for the constant chatter to cease, but eventually all eyes were on me. I was glad to see both Jill and Johnny in the crowd. "Thank you," I said after achieving near silence. "It has come to our attention an item from this museum was stolen this morning." There was collective grumble among the crowd as everyone began to talk again. "If I could get everyone's silence and cooperation, I would very much appreciate it!" I shouted over the crowd, which began to settle down again. "It is very important that I account for everyone here. You all signed in as you entered the museum this morning. When I call out your name, please raise your hand and walk into the adjacent room over there. Please be prepared to show some identification." Roll call went very smoothly as everyone on the list was accounted for.

The police arrived shortly thereafter and conducted both searches on each person and an exhaustive search of the museum. About an hour later, everyone was free to leave with apologies and a full refund for the inconvenience.

The days after the diamond was stolen were busy. I worked with the police and the museum head, pretending to help as much as I could to determine who was responsible for the stolen diamond. I had absolutely no contact with either Jill or Johnny other than a three-minute nighttime meeting. That was the plan.

We were all supposed to lie low until the investigation slowed down. It was a full week after the event before the museum reopened. It was another week before I would oversee the security system again. It was that day, yet another Friday, that I decided that the three of us should meet to retrieve the diamond from its hiding place.

I let Johnny know this at our preplanned nighttime meeting in the park. We planned to meet this upcoming Friday at seven o'clock in the morning in front of the museum. This was about an hour before I normally would begin work. I wanted to do this so close to my starting time because if anyone saw me, I would have a reason for being on the museum grounds. It's also over an hour before anyone else would likely be on the grounds.

Jill and Johnny walked up to the gates at seven o'clock sharp. We weren't going into the museum building. We only needed to get inside the gates and on the museum grounds where Johnny had hidden the diamond. There were only a few people across the street in the nearby park at this early hour. So, I was not concerned about arousing any suspicion as I unlocked the gates and three of us entered the grounds. I relocked the gates behind us.

I breathed in the crisp, cool morning air. The sun shone between a few clouds, which provided only a small amount of warmth. It was a tranquil morning. I felt this was a good omen.

Jill and Johnny were strangely quiet as we walked around the side of the museum building. "There's nothing to worry about," I said, whispering to them as we walked. I lifted a metal pail that I was carrying. "In case anyone sees us climbing the hill, we have an excuse for why we came." I looked over at Jill who seemed bothered by something. I don't think she even heard what I had said.

Jill reached into her jacket pocket and pulled out a newspaper as we walked. Jill shoved the newspaper in my face. "Explain that."

I shot her a confused look.

"Just read the paragraph we underlined old man," Johnny said.

I stopped walking for a moment and straightened out the paper as both Jill and Johnny eyed me. I found the underlined paragraph and read out loud, "Sources indicate that surveillance cameras were in working order during the heist. The police hope they will be the key to finding the culprit and the diamond."

"What kind of crap is that? Some camera may have gotten my picture. You said that Johnny could disconnect all the cameras."

The two had caught me off guard, which is a nice way of saying unprepared. I didn't like this feeling. I thought for a moment as I scratched my head. I turned to ask Johnny, "Did you cut the blue and red wires like I told you?"

"Of course, I did. Blue and red, not green."

"Alright then, we have nothing to worry about. You know, the press never knows what they're talking about."

"What if you're wrong?" Jill asked. "What if there was some other camera that got me on tape?"

"No," I said, shaking my head. "If that were true, you'd be behind bars by now. Wouldn't you?" Jill and Johnny looked at each other for a moment, pondering my question. "Come on! Let's get that diamond."

The museum was built about two hundred feet away from a very steep, rock-filled hill. There was a dirt trail that wound its way up the cliff-like hill. We began the slow climb. The last portion of the climb became treacherous, with nearly a sixty-degree grade toward the top. The loose gravel gave way under my feet several times sending me sprawling to the ground and sliding down the hill a bit. Each time I jumped right up, waving off any assistance from my compatriots. Finally, we reached the top.

While I paused to catch my breath, Johnny raced over to the water well. The kid had a seemingly endless source of energy. He began to tie a rope to himself so he could safely scale down the well. When the rope was secured around him and the outside rim of the well, Johnny tugged on it firmly to test it. He jumped up on the side of the well and said with a smile, "It's treasure time!"

Jill and I walked over to the well and shined flashlights as Johnny descended into the well. Even though the sun had risen, it wasn't high enough to provide much light down the well. Johnny fidgeted with several rocks embedded in the well's wall before pulling a large rock out. Jill and I exchanged smiles before we redirected the flashlight to shine on the safe.

Johnny sang repeatedly the phrase, "I've been working on my retirement, all the live-long day," as he slowly began turning the combination knob of the safe that we had built in the well. He opened the safe and stopped singing. The silence seemed to concern Jill, who stretched her neck out over the well to try to get a better view of what was going on. "I got it!" Johnny said before quickly climbing up the well. Before I knew it, he leaped out of the well and onto the ground.

"Let me see," Jill said with a smile. She held the diamond up to the sky with admiration. Then, her facial expression changed. "This is weird, but this diamond looks a little different."

"Give it here," Johnny said before feeling the diamond. He handed the diamond back to Jill before pulling his gun out and pointing it at me. "Where's the real diamond old man?"

"What are you talking about? You're holding it."

"You take me for a fool," Johnny said. "This is little lighter than the one I stole. You must have come up here and switched the real diamond with a fake."

Jill snickered. "You know, the original plan was to take the diamond from you, but not kill you. But, now that you tried to pawn off a fake diamond on us, maybe we should kill you."

Pressing the gun to the side of my head, Johnny said, "I'm going to give you until the count of ten. If you don't tell me where the real diamond is, I swear I'll blow your head off."

My mouth went dry as I was too afraid to move a muscle. I couldn't even speak.

Johnny began counting. When he reached five, I yelled, "Okay, okay! I admit I haven't been exactly straight with you two."

"Ah ha," Johnny said, moving the gun away from my head, but keeping it aimed at me. "Sometimes it takes a gun to make an honest man, doesn't it?"

"I didn't switch the diamonds, but I did mislead you on the wires. The green wire didn't set off the alarm. I mean if it did, then the suspicion would be directed toward me, right? I mean, how would robbers know to cut the blue and red, but not the green. They'd know it was an inside job."

"If cutting the green wire wouldn't have set off the general alarm, what's its purpose?" Jill asked.

"The green wire controls the surveillance cameras," I said.

"Then why didn't you tell me to cut that wire!" Johnny screamed. As his hand shook, the gun bobbed up and down.

"Insurance," I said. "I needed some kind of leverage against you two in case one of you stole the diamond." I then turned and looked at Johnny who took a step back but still kept the gun pointing at me. "Or in case one of you pulled a gun on me."

"You're too smart for your own good," Johnny said, taking another step away from me.

"It turns out the press was right. The cameras were working. The surveillance cameras caught both you and Jill doing your dirty work."

"Then why ain't we in jail?" Jill asked.

"Because I took the tapes catching you guys and replaced them with tapes with just snow," I said. "The tapes are now with a trusted friend. If anything happens to me, the tapes will be sent to the police and you two will be sent to prison, for life perhaps."

"You double crossed us," Johnny said under his breath.

"I protected myself. If nothing happens to me, you two are safe. Now, put the gun down and let me look at the diamond. I can tell you for sure if it's real or fake."

Johnny sighed deeply before dropping the gun down to his waist. Jill handed me the diamond and I looked it over carefully. "It looks a little different in natural light than in a museum," I said. "I think it's the real thing, but I need to take it back to my place to be sure."

"No one's going anywhere, yet," Jill said. "I'm going to take a look by the edge of the hill and see if there's any evidence of other fresh footprints. Keep your eye on him." Jill walked away, leaving me alone with Johnny.

"Give me back the diamond," Johnny said, reaching out with his free left hand.

I handed it to him. "You know, we're in this together, so you might as well put that gun away. If anything happens to me, you and your wife go to jail forever."

Johnny smiled before slowly putting the gun back in his holster. I took a few steps toward the well and looked down. "You know, maybe we should get the safe out of the wall. We can dust it for prints at my house. That will tell us for sure if someone other than you came back here."

"Not a bad idea," Johnny said, peering down the well. I acted quickly. I picked up the pail on the ground and brought it down hard on the back of his head. Knocked out, Johnny fell to the ground with a thud. I took his gun and then raced to hide behind a nearby tree and waited.

About two minutes later, Jill came back. "Johnny!" she shrieked, racing toward her fallen husband. When she bent down to check on him, I snuck up on her and once again slammed the pail against another skull.

The adrenaline ran quickly through my body so I didn't pause. I took the fake diamond out of Johnny's pocket. Then, I had to make their deaths appear to be accidental. I grabbed Johnny's body and dragged it to the edge of the steep hill. I pushed his body off the edge. I grabbed Jill's body and did the same. Finally, I threw the pail down the hill. I then raced to the other side of the hill, descended and walked back to the front of the museum where I called the police from a pay phone.

The police arrived within minutes and I directed them to the bodies that lay dead on the steep hillside. After emergency personnel tended to the bodies, Sheriff Paul Rosen took me down to the station for my official statement.

I had known Paul for over twenty years. We had fished, hunted, and most importantly, worked together over the years. I had helped him in so many cases. Ten years my junior, he always had an appreciation for my insight and ideas. Over the years, I had earned his respect and trust. At the station, Paul pulled out an audio recording device and set it on the table.

"Just procedure," Paul said before asking me what happened.

"Well, I arrived early for work today. I must have gotten in around seven o'clock. A couple said they heard there was a water well on top of the hill behind the museum. They begged me to let them in. Said they wanted to taste 'some real country water'. They had a pail and everything."

"So let me get this straight," Paul said, reading his notes. "The couple didn't want to get inside the building?"

"No," I said, shaking my head. "The guy, he uh, what was his name?" I asked, snapping my fingers as I looked up at the ceiling.

"According to his ID, his name was Jack Andersen," Paul said, looking down at a file. "They must have been married or siblings, cuz the little lady's name was Andersen also."

"I see," I said slowly. "Well, anyway, they were only interested in getting water. When they were near the top of that steep cliff, I happened to look up at them. I saw the guy fall backward, hitting his head pretty badly and roll down the hill. I think when the woman looked back she must have lost her footing, cuz she fell too."

"This is important. You're sure that you didn't see anyone else on that hill. Someone who might have caused the couple to fall."

"You mean foul play? Paul, I saw the fall. I can assure you they both just slipped. It was clearly an accident."

Paul turned off the recording device and stood up and thanked me for my time.

The next morning I read the newspaper that reported the terrible accident involving two hikers. The article quoted the sheriff's press release that stated, "Jack and Jill went up the hill to fetch a pail of water. Jack fell down and broke his crown and Jill came tumbling after." I snickered to myself as I caressed the real diamond in my hand and whispered, "A perfect crime."

Pay Up

"Pay up!" Big Vinny said with a crooked smile from the other side of the table. He picked up his cigar and wedged it in the side of his mouth. I looked down at my very meager stack of cash, trying to figure a way out of this. Big Vinny, a large man with more chins than a Chinese phone book, motioned with his hand for me to pay.

"I can't pay you right now," I said, looking at him with a stiff upper lip.

He chuckled as he looked at his thinner pal Jeremy next to him at the table, then turned back toward me and shook his head. "I don't think so."

"Give me a break," I said. "Times have been tough." Jeremy pretended to play an invisible violin.

"Pay now or else," Big Vinny said.

"Or else what?"

Big Vinny gestured with his right index finger toward his fat neck and moved it horizontally while saying, "kkkcckk." Big Vinny and Jeremy snickered wildly. I fell back in my chair, flashing back to how a bright man wound up in financial peril and in debt to the dim-witted Big Vinny. It had to be luck. Real bad luck…

I learned long ago that the key to financial success was through real estate. My goal was simple: economic domination. Back in the day when a dollar could actually buy something, I gathered up all the cash that I had to purchase my first piece of property. It was in a poor part of town near the railroad tracks. It wasn't much, but it was a start.

I wasn't about to stop there. In addition to earning a steady paycheck from a bank, I traveled around in my car looking for good real estate at fair prices. I shrewdly purchased some unimproved property at a bargain price. This land, located in an upscale neighborhood, was cheaper than expected since it was next door to a large water plant. Undaunted, I spent much of my savings, building a luxurious house on the property.

What seemed like a risk, paid off big time. I rented out the house to travelers who were willing to pay high daily rates. I used the steady cash flow from this rental to finance several other property purchases. I was truly on a roll and life simply couldn't have been better. Every chance I took was paying off. But, my luck was about to change.

I was thrown in jail on trumped up charges that I still don't understand. Without a steady paycheck while in jail, money started to get tight. Then, real estate and luxury taxes obliterated my savings.

By the time I got out of jail, I was forced to sell several properties, including the very first property that I had purchased. Not nearly ready to give up, I took several trips looking for good property to buy. Unfortunately, most properties were no longer for sale and my costs mounted, as I had to pay big dollars for a night's stay at several motels. Finally, I was forced to sell my cash cow, the property near the water plant. I was now without savings and I was living from $200 paycheck to $200 paycheck.

My last and fatal mistake was when I pulled my car up to Big Vinny's house, located in a ritzy area along the waterfront.

"So you're going to pay up or not?" Big Vinny asked, breaking my flashback. "Well?"

I sighed heavily before shaking my head.

Pay Up

Big Vinny smiled. "If you can't pay for your stroll on my Boardwalk, that means that it's the end for you. You lose." Jeremy mockingly waved goodbye.

I stood up from the table and looked at my watch. "Fine," I said, throwing my hands up in the air before silently vowing never to spend four hours playing Monopoly again.

Someone is Trying to Kill Me

"Are you Robert Douglas, the private eye?" the elderly woman asked with a terrified look on her pale face. I answered her with a nod. Her cold, clammy hands grabbed mine as she said, "Someone is trying to kill me."

Stunned, I stared at her for a moment. The woman's hands were shaking. Still a little startled myself, I asked her to sit down. As a precaution, I drew the blinds on the large window of my ground floor office and then locked my front door. I walked back to my desk and pulled out one of my standard form papers. "Your name, ma'am?"

"Margaret Wilson," the woman said, clutching her purse in her lap like a security blanket.

"Ms. Wilson. Who's trying to kill you?"

"I don't know."

"Hmm," I said, scratching my head. "Well, uh, why would anyone want to kill you?"

"I don't know," Margaret said, her eyes widened.

"What makes you think that someone wants to kill you?"

She thought about her answer for a moment. "I just have a feeling."

I groaned out loud and thought, "Not another one of *these* cases." I looked at her. "You don't know why someone would kill you. And you don't know who is trying to kill you. You don't even have a reason to believe your life is in danger."

"You've got to believe me. I need your help."

"Ma'am, I don't think there's anything to help you with," I said, rising.

Margaret jumped up and grabbed my hand again. "Please. I'll pay you a hundred dollars an hour."

I slowly sat back down. "What do you want me to do?"

"Be at my house tomorrow," the woman said, handing me a card. "I must go. I'll see you tomorrow morning at eleven." She began walking toward the door before suddenly stopping. "I don't want anybody at the house to know that you're a private eye. So tell anyone who asks you that you're a nephew of a friend of mine."

"Okay," I said, looking down at her card that read: Wilson Paintings, 253 Fairway Road, (803) 555-7439. Still looking down, I said, "I'm going to need to know more…" My words trailed off as I looked up and realized that she was gone. I walked over to the window and opened the blinds, just in time to see her get in the driver's seat of a black Mercedes and speed away.

The next morning I pulled my sputtering brown car up to 253 Fairway Road. My old car appeared woefully out of place in the upscale neighborhood. I waved to a jogger whose jaw dropped at the sight of my vehicle. In my fifties now, I stopped being self-conscious a long time ago.

Her house was an impressive, gated mansion. I marveled at the beautiful estate as I drove the car to the front gate. I pushed a button next to the speaker.

"May I help you?" a voice from the speaker asked.

"I'm Robert Douglas. I'm here to see Margaret Wilson."

There was a momentary pause. "Yes, Ms. Wilson is expecting you. Pull your car up to the end of the driveway."

The gates opened. I cautiously drove into the estate as the gates closed behind me.

As I drove up the long driveway, I admired the perfectly trimmed lawn, swimming pool, small greenhouse, tennis court, and large pond. As I brought the car to a halt at the end of the driveway, Margaret and an older man greeted me. The slender man was dressed in black slacks with a white-collared shirt. His short hair was almost entirely gray. He appeared meticulously neat and maintained a serious expression on his face.

"I'm so glad that you could make it," Margaret said, walking over to me. "This is James, our butler and a dear friend of mine."

"Your coat and hat sir?" James said, holding out his right hand. I was a little startled. No one had ever asked for my coat or hat before. That is, unless they wanted to borrow it. "Sir?" James said, breaking my trance. I slowly handed him my coat and hat. He tried to brush some dust off my coat as he headed back toward the house.

I took a step toward the house, but Margaret grabbed my arm. She had quite a grip for a woman her age. She waited a moment for James to be out of earshot before saying softly, "Remember when I told you someone is trying to kill me." I nodded my head slowly. "Well, now I'm sure of it. It's going to happen tomorrow night."

"How do you know that? And what makes you so sure?"

She looked around before saying, "Let's go into my room. It's safer there."

I followed Margaret into the house and up the stairs to her large bedroom. The rooms were lavishly furnished and the walls were decorated with beautiful artwork. The house was pristinely clean and not even a cushion appeared to be out of place. When we entered her bedroom, there was a young, pretty woman dusting.

"I was just straightening up your room, Miss Wilson," the woman said. Although her stature was on the smaller side, she seemed taller because she stood with her chest stuck out like a proud peacock.

"That's okay," Margaret said. "But Cathy, I will be using this room now."

"Yes ma'am," Cathy said before slowly exiting the room.

Margaret closed the door behind her and walked across the room to sit on the bed. She motioned for me to sit next to her before whispering, "Someone is trying to kill me."

I began to get frustrated. "You've told me that, but who is trying to kill you?"

"I don't know," Margaret said, reaching into her purse. "That's what I'm paying you for." She counted out $300 in twenty dollar bills. "You'll stay for three hours today."

"Okay," I said, taking the money. "But, I'm still not sure what you want me to do."

"Find out who's trying to kill me," Margaret said as if it were obvious. Margaret seemed more excited than afraid. Last night, she definitely looked scared. But today it felt like she thought this was more like a game.

"Wait a minute. Tell me again what makes you think someone is trying to kill you. You think it'll happen tomorrow?"

"Yes. I've had this feeling a long time that someone around here would like to kill me. Then, last night I picked up the phone and someone was already talking on the other end of the line. They said they were coming over tomorrow night to take care of me."

"Who said that?"

"I don't know, but it was the person on the line outside of this house."

"Who was on the line in *this* house?" I asked.

"I wouldn't know. I hung up immediately after I heard the person say that."

"Do you have any idea who would have been in the house at that time?"

"Everyone, I would guess," Margaret said as I got my pencil and small notepad out. "James is a live-in butler so I know he was here. I don't think Cathy would have left yet. And my oldest son Brad and his wife were definitely here." I continued to scribble on my small notepad. I immediately looked up when Margaret stopped talking, lifting my eyebrows. She said with a slight shoulder shrug, "That's everyone."

I was finding all of this too much to swallow. I got up from the bed and paced the room a little before stopping to ask, "Why did you choose to come to me rather than your family?"

"Isn't it obvious? I can't trust anyone in my family, especially after that phone call."

"What about friends? Why didn't you go to one of them?"

"What friends?" Margaret said, seemingly annoyed with my questions. "I haven't had any friends since my husband died."

I thought for a moment. "Do you have a will?" She slowly nodded her head. "Who's seen it?"

"Nobody but me and my lawyer. Why do you ask?"

"Well, you obviously are very wealthy," I said, putting my pad back in my pocket. "I've seen large inheritances as motives for murder."

"But I barely have any money. This is my oldest son's estate, not mine."

I felt like tearing my hair out. None of the things Margaret was saying made any sense. She said she believes that someone is trying to kill her based on some phone call. But why? And who?

"Margaret. Tell me word for word what the person said when they said they would take care of you."

"The person said, 'I am going to take care of Margaret Friday night."

"That's what they said? That could mean anything. It probably doesn't mean someone wants to kill you."

"Listen to me," Margaret said, grabbing my arm with a surprisingly tight grip. "I know the tone the person was using. It wasn't friendly." Margaret appeared frightened again. She slowly let go of my arm, seemingly embarrassed at how she had grabbed me.

"I've got an idea. I know a way to tell if anyone is really out to kill you." Margaret listened closely as I glanced at my pad. "I'll announce that I'm going to take you out of state tomorrow in front of your son, his wife, James, and Cathy."

"Why?"

"If anyone really has plans for your death tomorrow, that person will object to you leaving," I said. I hoped this would prove to Margaret that she had let her imagination go wild and she was not in any danger. When no one cared whether she left, it should calm her nerves. After all, if I could make her feel better by proving that this was all in her imagination, I would have earned my money.

Margaret shrugged her shoulders. "Well, let's try it."

Margaret and I walked downstairs and into the living room where a man and a woman were relaxing. Sitting at a table, the man was playing by himself with an electronic chessboard. He appeared to have one eye on the chessboard and the other buried in a book which was titled "How to Play Winning Chess." The man, who wore eyeglasses, had wavy, black hair with small touches of gray.

The woman was relaxing on the sofa reading the business section of the daily paper. It appeared she was reviewing the stock quotes. She had a wicked smile on her face so I would guess that she was pleased with her stocks' performance. Probably helped with expensive plastic surgery, the woman's attractive face was devoid of wrinkles. Her neck and ears were covered in sparkling jewelry that I guessed cost a small fortune.

"I have an announcement to make," Margaret said. Brad and Rebecca looked at each other uneasily as Margaret called James and Cathy outside. Margaret then said to the group, "Robert and I are going to St. Louis tonight to visit my friend Beverly. We'll be back in three days."

There was complete silence as everyone in the room looked at each other. I studied their faces as I anxiously awaited their response. Rebecca was the first to speak. "Um, mom. This is so sudden. Do you think that is such a good idea?"

Margaret's and my eyes met as a chill went up my spine. "Why wouldn't I?" Margaret asked. "My friend was just released from the hospital."

"I agree with Rebecca," Brad said. "Give her a call, but it's silly to go all the way to St. Louis tonight. That's a long drive."

"I don't want to call her. I want to be with her." I was amazed with Margaret's acting ability. She seemed totally engrossed in the part.

"Margaret," James said, walking up to her. "You probably should stay here. I know Beverly would understand. I'll try to ring her now if you give me the phone number."

"I don't think Margaret wants to call her," I said, stepping in between James and Margaret.

Cathy took a few steps toward Margaret before saying, "James and I are fixing a fine meal tomorrow for dinner. Your favorite."

"I don't understand," I said. "Why is everyone against her visiting a sick friend?"

"I've heard enough of this silliness," Brad said, rising from his chair. He walked over to Margaret. "I love you, but I don't want you to go anywhere tomorrow night. Maybe we can arrange it for later in the week." Brad kissed her on the cheek before leaving the room.

"Listen to Brad," Rebecca said. "Believe me. He's doing what's best for you." Rebecca rushed out of the room, presumably to catch up to Brad.

James and Cathy slowly walked back to the kitchen to finish lunch. "I told you," Margaret said, looking me dead in the eye. "One of them wants me here tomorrow night, to kill me."

"One of them?" I said perplexed. "They *all* at least want you here tomorrow night." My plan had backfired. Instead of erasing her fears, I had added to them. "Your family sure is acting strange. To be on the safe side, maybe you should leave the house tomorrow night."

"What would that solve? I'll just be killed when I return."

I scratched my head and my eyes squinted as I began to feel a little uncomfortable. "Even still, I think..."

"No. I'm not leaving. The only way I will be able to solve this is for us to stay and catch the killer. I just want my peace of mind back. My gosh, I want to trust my family again."

"Alright," I said, readying myself for the upcoming task. "We'll stay. I'm going to find out what's going on around here. I promise."

I started looking around upstairs. I didn't really know what I was looking for, but since Margaret was paying a hundred bucks an hour, I felt I should at least look like I was busy. Only two doors down the hall, I saw James quickly duck into a side room. I raced down the hall and caught the door just before it shut. Peering into the room, I couldn't see James through the crack of the door. I slowly opened the door.

The room was full of spectacularly beautiful paintings. James had his back to me admiring one of the nicer paintings, a stunning display of red and orange in a portrait of the sun setting over the horizon. There were several easels, three chairs, a couple of tables, and white sheets covering the floor. I could tell my snooping skills were rusty when I tripped over an empty paint can.

James quickly turned around. "What are you doing Mr. Douglas?"

"Just taking a look around. Real nice house." James simply stared at me as if he was trying to ascertain if I was telling the truth. I felt a strong urge to break the uncomfortable silence. "Who bought all of these paintings?"

"Nobody. Margaret refuses to sell them."

"Wow! These are Margaret's paintings. This artwork is spectacular."

"Look at this painting," James said, pointing to the painting of the sunset. "If she would take it to an established auction house, with Margaret's reputation as a painter, she could net $10,000, minimum."

"No kidding. How do you know that?"

"I used to spend a lot of time at auction houses." James let out a deep sigh. "But she insists on letting them collect dust. She has over 200 paintings in storage. She hasn't tried to sell a painting in the last four years. I can't understand it unless it's some type of business decision."

"Business decision?"

"Yeah, paintings from an established painter like Margaret will go for almost double the price after her death because of the inherent limitation on future paintings."

"You think Margaret is delaying selling most of her paintings so her heirs can gain a higher selling price."

"I know it sounds strange, but if she could net additional..." James paused to apparently do some calculations in his head. "Um, six hundred grand."

"Wow! That much?"

"Sure. And that's just the incremental amount with her death. I'd figure she'd be able to sell all of her artwork for about 1.2 million. I better get back to fixing lunch. This door locks automatically when you leave. So please don't leave anything in here." Before I could say a word, James exited the room.

About five minutes after James left, I heard some rattling of keys at the door of the painting room. I quickly hid under a nearby table. I peered out from underneath the tablecloth to see Cathy open the door with her key. "What was Cathy doing in here?" I thought to myself. She walked over to a stack of paintings on the table adjacent to the one I was under.

"Boy, the old lady can really paint," Cathy said, admiring a painting. "This is going to make me rich." She then looked in my direction and spotted me. "What are you doing down there?"

"Looking for my contacts," I said, not expecting her to believe any excuse I would be able to come up with. I got up from underneath the table. "How long have you worked here?"

"Almost a month. Why?"

"Only a month and Margaret let you have the keys to a room full of valuable paintings."

"I don't know what you are insinuating but I'm a trustworthy person," Cathy said. "Besides what makes you think they're so valuable? They're sure nice, but there are a lot more valuable items in this house."

"You sure about that?"

"I don't know," Cathy said defensively as she folded her arms in front of her chest. "If they were so valuable, I'm sure Miss Wilson would have sold them by now, right?" Cathy stared at me as if she was expected me to answer but I didn't. "Well, I must be getting downstairs."

I followed Cathy downstairs and outside to the back patio. Margaret, Brad, and Rebecca were already sitting at a round table next to the pool. A long table nearby was filled with a buffet. I fixed my plate, sat down and ate with Margaret, Brad, and Rebecca.

Over lunch, I learned that Brad and Rebecca are sole owners of Italianos, a trendy, upscale Italian restaurant. Although I have never been there, I was familiar with the popular, local restaurant. I had heard once that you needed to secure reservations at least two weeks in advance to eat there.

Interested in Brad and Rebecca's background to be successful restaurant owners, I peppered them with a lot of questions over lunch. I learned that Brad, an accomplished chef, worked the operations side of the restaurant. He created the menu and trained employees in every aspect of the business. Rebecca, as CEO of the company, handled all financial aspects of the business.

"You aren't leaving to visit Beverly tomorrow night, right?" Brad asked. He shoved a spoon full of chicken salad in his mouth and chewed slowly as he awaited an answer.

"I decided to stay," Margaret said. "I just talked to Beverly on the phone. She's doing better."

"Good," Brad said with a smile. He turned toward me. "Would you like to have dinner with us tomorrow night?"

"Yes, do come," Margaret said.

"I'd love to come," I said.

After lunch, Margaret and I walked back upstairs to her room alone. I hadn't gathered a whole lot of information from my informal talks. The little information that I did get only made me have more questions for Margaret.

"Well, what did you find out? Who's trying to kill me?"

"I don't know, but I have a few questions for you."
Margaret's forehead wrinkled as she seemed surprised and
maybe even annoyed that I was asking her questions. "Why
aren't you selling any of your paintings?"

"What do my paintings have to do with trying to find the
killer?"

"Maybe a whole lot. If you die, your paintings will be worth
more. The murderer would be able to get a lot more when he or
she sold them."

"That's silly. The murderer wouldn't be able to sell
something that's not his."

"But what if the murderer thought he or she would inherit
the paintings after your death."

"Wow, I never thought of that," Margaret said. I expected
her to be stunned or possibly upset when I suggested this.
Instead, she seemed intrigued with the idea.

"Now," I said, looking down at my notes. "You mentioned
that you have a will that only you and your lawyer have seen."
Margaret nodded in agreement. "Since no one in your family
actually knows the details of your will, the key question is who
thinks they will be included in the will?"

"I see what you mean. The people who think they would
inherit the most would be the suspects." I was shocked by how
intrigued Margaret seemed at the idea that someone in her
household could be a killer. "Well, my three children would
expect to be included in the will. You met Brad. He's the
oldest. Then, there's my daughter Sandra and my youngest child
Dennis."

"Do you think Rebecca, Cathy, or James would expect to be
included in your will?"

"Cathy just started working here so she wouldn't expect
anything at all. I don't think Rebecca would expect anything
directly, but remember she is married to my oldest son. And
James, he wouldn't…" Margaret paused in mid sentence as she

appeared to stare off in the distance. "Actually, I have known James a long time. He might well expect something."

"Hmff!" I said, scratching my head. "That didn't eliminate anybody, except maybe Cathy."

How time flies when you are having fun. My three hours were about to come to a close. I was unclear what, if anything, I had accomplished. Luckily, Margaret was satisfied with my work enough that she requested that I come back at four o'clock tomorrow. I would be a bodyguard and she wanted me to be armed. To be honest, I knew I wasn't taking any risk at all. No one was planning to kill Margaret. She had obviously let her imagination get away from her. Part of me felt bad about taking this woman's money when I knew she was not in any danger. However, I rationalized it by telling myself that I was giving her peace of mind, which had to be worth something.

The next afternoon I was back at the gates in front of the Wilson Estate. "I'm here to see Margaret. It's Robert Douglas."

"Yes, I can tell by your automobile sir," James said as the gates opened.

When I brought my car to a halt inside the gates, James was waiting for me. Margaret raced out of the house toward my car to greet me. I can't explain it. Even though I knew she would be okay, I was slightly relieved to see her. I got out of the car and handed James my coat and hat before he even asked.

"First things first," Margaret said, reaching in her purse. She quickly counted out three hundred dollars. "That will cover the first three hours." As I put the money in my pocket, I noticed Cathy watching from an upstairs window. When she saw me look up, she quickly disappeared.

"Well," I said, taking a deep breath. "Who's here?"

"Just Brad, Rebecca, Cathy, and James," Margaret answered.

"That means whoever was supposed to come over hasn't come yet," I said in deep thought. "Why don't you lock yourself in your room for a little while?"

Margaret wanted to stay with me, but I convinced her that I could learn more if she wasn't around. Besides, the safest place for her was locked in her room.

After seeing Margaret to her room, I wandered around upstairs until I heard some noise behind a closed door. There were two voices. I pressed my ear up against the door.

"I want 50% of the excess or I'll expose you," an angry female voice said.

"Be reasonable," another female voice said.

"Look, I want at least ten thousand tonight," the first voice said, slightly louder.

"Shh!" the other voice said. "Be quiet." The two women began talking considerably softer. I pressed my ear up against the door further.

"Excuse me Mister Douglas." James startled me as I jumped away from the door. "What are you doing?"

"Doing?" I said, walking away from the door and leading him down the hall. "I'm not really doing anything. Just exploring the house."

"You're quite a snooper," James said as we reached the top of the stairs. "First the painting room, now this." He looked at me straight in the eye as if he was trying to figure something out. "I'm not sure what you're doing here, but be careful. The Wilsons deal harshly with thieves."

Before I could respond, James had turned and walked away. I slowly walked down the stairs, thinking about the conversation that I had overheard. As I entered the living room, I could hear Brad's voice coming from behind a closed door. I looked around to see if James was in view. He wasn't so I once again pressed my ear up against the door.

"Now, I want you two here right at five o'clock," Brad said. There was a pause in which I could not hear any sounds. "No, don't worry about Margaret. She doesn't suspect a thing. I gotta go. Just don't be late. Bye."

I raced back to the living room, shocked to see Margaret walking down the stairs. "What are you doing? You're supposed to be locked in your room."

"I know, but I was wondering what you were doing."

"Let's go somewhere we can talk in private," I said a little frustrated.

Margaret led me into a room which resembled a study. As soon as she closed the door, I said, "I overheard Brad talking to two people on the phone. They're coming over at five o'clock tonight." I looked at my watch. "That's thirty minutes from now. I'm not sure why they're coming, but you…"

"They're coming to kill me?"

"I doubt that's the case," I said, grabbing Margaret's hand. "But just in case, I think it's best you stay locked in your room. And this time, stay there."

As I watched Margaret go back upstairs, I was actually worried about her for the first time. In my heart, I still believed all this was some weird coincidence. But still, what if it wasn't? What if someone was really coming in about a half an hour to kill her? "Robert," a voice said behind me. I turned around and saw Brad and James.

"I'd like to have a word with you," Brad said to me. He then turned to James. "Thank you. You've been most helpful." James dipped his head toward Brad before walking away.

I followed Brad into the same study in which Margaret and I had just been. "Have a seat Mister Douglas," Brad said, pointing to a small wooden chair. As I sat down, Brad walked around the huge desk and sat down on the large swivel chair. Brad rested his hands on the desk, clasping his fingers together, and looked at me.

"You wanted to talk to me?" I said, breaking the awkward silence.

"James told me that you have been acting suspicious. So I called Beverly just a moment ago. She has never heard of a Robert Douglas."

A shot of nervous adrenaline pulsated through my body. "I can explain that," I said, thinking of an explanation.

"I'm listening," Brad said, folding his arms in front of his chest as he waited.

"I'm here on business."

"What kind of business?"

"I can't say."

"That does it," Brad said rising. "I want you off the premises right now."

"Hold on!" I said also getting to my feet. "I'm a private eye. I'm here to investigate. Margaret thinks someone is going to kill her, tonight."

Brad started to laugh as he fell back into his chair. I expected disbelief, maybe a little concern, but not laughter. "Is that what she told you? And you believed her?"

"Is there some reason that I shouldn't?"

"Well, this is the fourth time that she has done this in the last year and a half. She needs excitement in her life. So she tells people someone is trying to kill her or she needs to find her long lost son."

"You sound so sure of yourself."

"Experience breeds assurance. Trust me. No one's gonna kill Margaret."

"I have a question then. If nothing is going to happen to Margaret tonight, why was everyone so insistent on her being here?"

"Alright. I guess I can tell you. We're throwing Margaret a surprise birthday party. Her other son and daughter will be here in less than fifteen minutes. That's why she has to be here. Now, how much is my mother paying you?"

"A hundred dollars an hour," I said, feeling guilty.

"A hundred dollars an hour! This is becoming an expensive hobby." Brad got up and walked around the desk. He sat on top of the edge of the desk, his eyes trained on me. "I'll make you a deal. If you promise not to take any more money from my mother, you can stay for the party."

"Deal," I said, shaking his hand.

"They'll be here soon. Please stay with my mother upstairs so we can set up the surprise downstairs."

I walked back upstairs to Margaret's room. I tried to open the door, but it was locked. I knocked on the door. Margaret opened the door and I walked in. She quickly closed the door behind me.

I couldn't help but laugh. "You know, it does no good to lock your door if you're going to open it to anyone who knocks."

"I suppose you're right, but what did you find out?"

"I found out who your five o'clock visitors are." Because Margaret was so clearly on edge, I felt it was best that she was not caught completely off guard with her children's visit. She moved a few feet closer to me, apparently intensely interested in my next sentence. "They're your children Dennis and Sandra, but they aren't coming to kill you. They're just coming to visit."

"Just to visit? I don't believe that. Sandra hasn't visited me in over three years and I haven't even spoken to Dennis in the last five years."

"Five years?"

"Yes," Margaret said, nodding her head. "Dennis and I haven't spoken since his father died. And Sandra, we only talk about twice a year."

I walked over to the window and saw a car coming up the driveway. "You have to trust me. Everything is going to be ok."

Margaret put her hand over her heart as she stared at the floor. She still looked very concerned.

"Mom!" Brad exclaimed, outside of Margaret's bedroom door. "I need you to come downstairs."

"Come on, let's at least go down and meet them," I said, lightly tapping her knee. "You'll be fine. I'll be with you."

Margaret thought a moment before clutching my hand in a tight grip. We slowly exited the room and followed Brad downstairs.

"Surprise!" everyone yelled as Margaret entered the dining room. She must have jumped two feet in the air as the sudden outburst nearly scared her to death. I surmised that the two new faces in the room were Margaret's younger children, Dennis and Sandra. Dennis had a boyish face and curly black hair. With what appeared to be a nervous smile, Dennis stood farthest from the stairs with his hands clasped together near his waist. Sandra, who was clearly older than Dennis, had shoulder length brown hair. Sandra, along with others, clapped loudly as she walked toward us.

Sandra was the first to hug Margaret, followed by Rebecca and Brad.

"Mom," Dennis said, approaching her. "Can we talk alone?"

Margaret looked at me as if to ask if it was alright. I motioned with my hand for her to go ahead. As they left the room, Rebecca walked over to a smiling Brad and kissed him. "Let's give her our present now."

"The present!" Brad said, pushing Rebecca away. "I forgot to pick it up this morning." Brad looked at his watch. "I'll go pick it up now." He raced out of the dining room.

"Where's the nearest powder room?" Sandra asked. "I think I've forgotten it's been so long."

"Down the hallway near the front door on the right," Rebecca said. After Sandra left, Rebecca walked over to me. We were the only two left in the room. "Brad told me that you aren't really Beverly's nephew."

"Sorry to deceive you. In my defense, it was Margaret's idea."

"I'm not surprised," Rebecca said.

A few minutes later, James walked in. "Where is everybody?"

"Margaret and Dennis are talking," Rebecca responded to James. "Sandra's in the bathroom and Brad went to pick up Margaret's gift."

"Really," James said. "His car is still out front."

"He must have taken mine then. Oh gosh. I forgot to pick up the cake."

"I'll get it if you like ma'am."

"That's okay," Rebecca said, tapping James on the shoulder. "I'll get it. You keep an eye on dinner." Rebecca hurried out of the room.

"Have you seen Cathy lately?" James asked me.

"Actually no," I said, trying to remember the last time that I saw her.

"Hmmpf," James muttered, heading out of the room. "Just like Cathy to be missing, when she is needed most."

I was alone in the dining room. I felt a little strange because I did not feel that I was needed here. I saw the wine bottle and wine glasses on the table. I couldn't help but pour myself a glass.

"I don't think we've met," Sandra said, returning to the room. She startled me so much that I spilled a little of the wine. In the short time that we spoke, I found out that Sandra was a registered nurse for an inner city hospital.

"So what do you do for a living?"

"I'm a private eye."

"A private eye, eh," Sandra said with a smirk. "Tell me. What does it take to be a private eye?"

"A quick and observant mind." I glanced up and down Sandra's full figured body. "Like how you got traces of mud on your shoes on the way to the bathroom."

"Some detective you are," Sandra said, rolling her eyes. "If you look closely, you'd see the mud is dry. I must have gotten that in the dirt parking lot at the hotel we're staying at." Sandra folded her arms in front of her chest as if she was awaiting a reply.

Before I could respond, Margaret and Dennis walked back into the room. Both of them were smiling. Sandra asked Margaret if she could talk to her and the two left the room, leaving Dennis and me alone.

"I'm Dennis," he said, holding out his hand.

"Robert Douglas," I said before shaking hands. "Glad to see you and your mother reunited after all of these years.

"I kept wondering whether it was a mistake to come here. After talking to her, I think it was the smartest thing that I've ever done in my life."

Dennis and I chatted for about five more minutes. I found out that he was currently an unemployed actor still waiting for his big break. He obviously had the good looks for television or the big screen, which made me wonder if he had the matching acting skill. Dennis told me that he entered the acting profession despite Margaret's constant warnings that it was a "one in a million shot."

When Margaret and Sandra returned to the room, I began to feel very out of place. "I believe I should go," I whispered to Margaret.

"Hold on." Margaret turned and yelled toward the kitchen, "James!"

"Yes ma'am," James said as he entered the room.

"Could you please show Dennis and Sandra around the house? Give them the grand tour- inside and outside." James nodded and led Dennis and Sandra out of the room.

"Thank you for everything," Margaret said to me.

I reached into my pocket and pulled out two hundred of the original three hundred dollars that she gave me. "I only stayed one full hour."

Margaret seemed confused as she took the money. "I realize that I was wrong and I'm sorry that I dragged you down here, but I'd..."

"Don't be sorry. You were frightened and confused."

"I'd really like you to stay." I shot her a glare as I tilted my head. "As a friend, not as a bodyguard."

"I'd be delighted to stay as your friend if that's what you want."

Once Sandra and Dennis completed their tour, the four of us chatted for another fifteen minutes before Brad and Rebecca returned. Brad was carrying a large box. Rebecca patted Brad on the back as she said, "I saw Brad on the way home so I just followed him."

James entered the room. "Dinner is ready in the dining room." Then, he said to Brad in a lowered voice, "I looked all around the house. I still can't find Cathy. I had to prepare dinner by myself."

As everyone else headed toward the dining room, I could hear Brad tell James, "That's strange" before asking him to get Margaret's gift out of his car.

Dinner was delightful, the conversation interesting, and the company was superb. James brought in a birthday cake with a single candle, placing it in front of Margaret.

"At your age, we felt seventy candles might be too much for you," Brad said as everyone laughed. Margaret quickly blew out the candle which drew applause from the table.

As James cut the cake and handed everyone a slice, he said to Brad, "I looked on the side of the house. Cathy's car is gone. She must have left. That's why I couldn't find her anywhere."

"Really," Brad said, taking his first bite of the cake. "She knew we needed her the entire night."

"Why would she leave without telling anyone?" Rebecca asked.

James simply shrugged his shoulders. He turned to leave, but Margaret stopped him. "Will you stay and have a slice of cake too?"

"I'd be delighted."

Everyone finished off their slices of birthday cake about the same time when Brad stood up. "Fifty-five years ago today you married dad. The most treasured activity that you two shared was planting in your garden. That's why when you came to live with me, we constructed the greenhouse."

Brad sat back down and Sandra rose. "When I grew up, I remember you and dad would plant as the sun set. I heard on special days you still do that around seven o'clock."

"On the dot," Margaret said, starting to cry.

Sandra sat down and Dennis rose. "Our gift to you is a variety of beautiful, rare plants. And in long standing tradition, we would like you to plant them in the greenhouse at exactly seven o'clock tonight."

"It's already 6:55," Brad said, rising to his feet. "Let's get going."

Everyone walked out of the house and onto the back patio where a variety of small plants were. Margaret picked up one of the more exotic plants and began taking a step toward the greenhouse.

"Whooah!" Dennis said, grabbing a hold of his mother. "It's not seven yet. You can't leave until exactly seven o'clock."

Margaret turned to everyone. "Thank you so much. Will you allow me to plant this first plant in the greenhouse alone? I want to be alone with my husband's spirit."

"Of course," Brad said. Everyone followed with a chorus of "sure" and "whatever you like".

Margaret looked at Dennis' watch. "It's exactly seven o'clock." She walked into the greenhouse alone as everyone watched her with smiles on their faces.

She had been in the greenhouse for about five minutes. Everyone was silent during that time. I wasn't about to break that silence. I looked at everyone. Only great respect and forgiving love were shown on their faces. But then something broke the silence. Something broke the strong feeling of love. It was a loud, hateful sound. It was the sound of a huge explosion that blew the greenhouse into a million pieces.

Everyone stood motionless for what seemed like several minutes. A few jaws dropped in disbelief. A few heads shook in disgust. And a few tears fell in sorrow. Everything seemed so great just moments ago. Now, sheer horror had surfaced.

"No!" Sandra yelled. Her eyes widened and she placed her hand over her heart.

Rebecca was speechless, showing little emotion as she stared at what used to be the greenhouse. A plume of black smoke rose to the sky.

"Maybe she survived!" Dennis cried as he ran toward the greenhouse. Instinctively, everyone followed right behind him. I knew before we got half way that she hadn't. Dennis broke down on the ground sobbing when the realization hit him.

James called the police and the fire department as the five of us waited in the living room completely silent. Margaret's words kept ringing back to me "someone is trying to kill me." I thought she was just a crazy old lady. I wish I would have taken her more seriously. If I had, perhaps she would still be alive.

As we sat in the living room waiting, I was comforted by the fact that I had a good relationship with the local police department. It was a necessity to being a successful private eye. It's something that I have worked on for over seventeen years.

The result of my labor is a good working relationship and mutual respect for Deputy Michael Petersen. Petersen was a young, clean shaven officer with short black hair and a perfect smile. In his late twenties and a fan of working out at the gym, the handsome deputy was quite the heartthrob among young ladies in the town. Although extremely ambitious and a big believer of "following his heart", he was always aware of the chain of command.

Officer Petersen's boss was Sheriff William Drake. Standing over six feet tall, Sheriff Drake was a physically imposing man. Sporting a buzz haircut and a mustache, Sheriff Drake looked menacing when he was in a bad mood. A transplanted sheriff from another town a year ago, it has taken a little time for him to warm up to my unusual relationship with the department. However, with time, he came to respect me as a resource and has been willing to provide some assistance when I needed a favor on a client matter.

Four police officers in uniform entered the living room. I spotted Officer Petersen who walked in right next to Sheriff Drake. Taking control immediately, Sheriff Drake barked out orders to his men. He then turned and addressed the five of us. "Is everyone who is in this house in this room?"

"Yes," I said rising. I didn't get to know Margaret very well, but I liked her. It was now my mission to do everything I could to help the police find her murderer. "I was employed by the deceased and I..."

"Mister Douglas," Sheriff Drake said. "I'm sure you have a lot to tell me, but just sit down for now. I'll be asking a lot of questions. Just wait."

I clenched my fist tightly as I sat back down. After introducing himself, Sheriff Drake stated that he wanted to keep things very orderly and asked everyone to remain calm. After each of us gave him our names and relationship to Margaret, he asked for a recounting of the night's events, which Brad delivered.

"So who else knew that she would be going in the greenhouse at that seven o'clock?" Sheriff Drake asked.

"I knew," James said, raising his hand awkwardly. The sheriff looked at James with a raised eyebrow as he jotted a quick note down. "But so did Cathy," James quickly added. "We all discussed it when we were planning the party."

"Hold on a minute!" Sheriff Drake said, looking down at his notepad. "Who's Cathy? You guys told me that everyone was here."

"Everyone but Cathy," Rebecca said. "She left earlier in the day. She's our maid."

"I must admit it was a bit mysterious," James said. "She left without telling anyone. She still had work to do."

"I need the home number of this Cathy woman," Sheriff Drake said.

"I'll get it," James said as he got up to leave the room. He returned, holding up a small sheet of paper.

"Petersen," Sheriff Drake said to the younger officer. "Contact Cathy and get a statement on her version of events. In fact, see if she can come over here."

Officer Petersen nodded, took the note from James and left the room. A female uniformed officer bent down to speak to Sheriff Drake. She spoke softly, but because I was so near the two officers, I could pick up every word.

"What remains of the body has been sent down to the coroner's office."

"I suppose it's pretty bad," the sheriff said with a grimace on his face.

The female officer nodded. "Doubt a positive I.D. will be able to be made."

At that moment, Officer Petersen came back to the room. "Well, is Cathy coming over?" Sheriff Drake asked.

"No. She's not there. I left a message telling her to call the police at your office number."

My head was spinning. I was trying so hard to figure out exactly who killed Margaret. Well, it had to be either Cathy, Brad, Rebecca, James, Sandra, or Dennis. But why was she murdered? What was the motive? I could only think of those darn paintings. But there was a troubling paradox. The people who really had a chance to get the pictures in the will love her too much to have her killed for the money they would eventually get anyway when she died of natural causes. And those who didn't love her and might be crazy enough to kill her really had no chance to inherit the paintings.

"Mister Douglas!" Sheriff Drake said loudly. I was so deep in thought I had not heard him apparently say my name earlier. He wanted to question me alone about all of the events after Margaret hired me. After the discussion, I left my contact information with uniformed officers and was asked to leave.

Two days had passed since Margaret's death. Sitting at my desk in my office late in the afternoon, I stared at other client files, but my mind was still on Margaret's case. Even though it was the one case that would never yield further fees, I was obsessed with this case. And why was that? Possibly, because I liked Margaret and I wanted to know who did her harm. But, deep down, I knew that wasn't the reason. The reason was simple. I had failed in my job to protect her and I was filled with guilt. The only thing that could ease that guilt was to catch the killer.

Frustrated, I tossed the other client file across the room that I was pretending to read. Quickly growing tired, I rubbed my exhausted eyes in a vain attempt to help me refocus. I decided to reread an article in yesterday's newspaper for the fifth time. On page 3 of the local section of the paper, the headline read "Famous Painter Murdered in Own Home".

At that moment, I heard my front door open. I quickly looked up. It was Sheriff Drake, whom I hadn't seen since the night of the murder.

"Hi sheriff," I said, rising from my chair. He motioned with his hand for me to sit down. As I slowly sat back down, he took off his blue police jacket and sat down in one of the chairs facing my desk. "Any progress on finding Margaret's killer?"

"Some," Sheriff Drake said, remaining tight lipped. "Do you know what bothers me the most about this case?" He waited for me to shrug my shoulders before he continued, "Motive. What do you think the motive was?"

"I don't know," I replied with a sigh as I sunk deeper in my chair. I rested my chin in the palm of my hand, pausing to reflect. "I think it has something to do with all of those paintings and selling them for more after Margaret's death."

"Maybe. Look, we've worked with each other before so I'm going to cut to the chase. Did you ever have any contact with either Margaret or anyone else in that household before she came to visit you three days ago?"

"No," I said as my mind caught up to his train of thought. "I wasn't hired by anyone to harm Margaret."

"It's just with all the snooping around I was told that you were doing prior to the explosion, you would have had the opportunity to possib…"

"Everyone had an opportunity. What about Cathy? Where did she say she was all night? And why did she leave early?"

There was an awkward silence as it appeared he was weighing whether to share information with me. Finally, he said, "She didn't. We still haven't caught up with her. This morning we found her car at the airport. She must have skipped town."

"Maybe that's who you should be looking to interrogate," I said still upset with his inference.

"Don't worry," Sheriff Drake said, rising to his feet. "We'll find Cathy. Since you think money is the motive, I will share one piece of information with you. Margaret's only assets were those paintings and they were appraised at about $700,000. But, with her death, I hear they could go for double that."

"Wow! Who inherited them?"

"Except for one painting that went to James, the will designated all of them go to Brad."

My mouth dropped in shock as he turned to leave. "Wait a minute! Her other children, Sandra and Dennis didn't get anything in the will?"

"Not one red cent," Sheriff Drake replied.

I was up all night tossing and turning. Margaret's words of "someone is trying to kill me" kept ringing in my head. The more I thought about it, I wasn't really surprised at the will. She obviously made the will before Sandra and Dennis visited. They were still on bad speaking terms. So, naturally her only other son would get the bulk of the money. No one could have possibly murdered her expecting to inherit anything of any value except Brad.

So did Brad kill her for the money? I just can't accept that. He loved her. Why would he take care of her and support her for twenty years and then kill her for money that he would one day likely inherit anyway. Besides, why would Brad kill anyone for money? Judging from his estate, he already had more money than he knew what to do with.

Alright, what about Rebecca? Would she kill Margaret for the money that she was sure her husband would inherit. This was easier to believe, but still very, very unlikely. Like Brad, Rebecca was rolling in money. But equally important, I really believe that she liked Margaret. I'm a good judge of character and from what I saw, Rebecca truly loved her.

Then, there's James. I don't see how he gained at all from Margaret's death. For twenty years that he worked for her, they built quite a friendship. If he were going to kill her for some other reason, why did he wait twenty years? And what could Margaret ever do to make someone so mad that they would want to kill her?

And that brings me to Dennis and Sandra. Did Margaret do something to drive those two away? Or were they just ungrateful, uncaring children? Either way, would they come all the way out to kill Margaret after not visiting in years? I suppose it is possible, but hardly probable. I mean, they were out of her life already. Why kill her?

And I can't forget the missing Cathy. Why did she leave town so abruptly? I remember she was looking at the paintings the day Margaret was killed. She said something about them making her rich, which doesn't make any sense. She didn't try to steal them and she couldn't dream of inheriting them. Then, she disappears. Why did she leave town? If she did set that explosive to go off at seven o'clock because she knew that's when Margaret would be in there, that was the stupidest thing to do.

Things just didn't make sense. This case was like a jigsaw puzzle that someone had cut off corners of individual pieces with a pair of scissors.

I awoke the next morning groggy, probably because I was only able to get a few hours sleep. I showered, shaved and got dressed. I fixed myself some cold cereal and toast. As I ate, I read the newspaper. I nearly choked on my toast when I read the headline, "Bulk of Wilson Paintings to be Auctioned Off". Wow! Brad was wasting no time in cashing in on the money from the paintings. For some reason, it just seemed wrong. I thought he would have at least waited until the murder investigation was completed. Then again, I bet the bidding price would be even higher when there is suspicion of foul play in the painter's death. I couldn't put my finger on it, but there was something fishy about Brad's decision. I decided to race down to the police station and make sure Sheriff Drake was aware of Brad's latest move.

I walked into Sheriff Drake's office. His desk was almost completely covered in papers. "Have you seen this?" I asked, throwing the newspaper on his desk.

"What about it?" he asked with a heavy sigh. I don't think he appreciated the interruption.

"The article to the right. Brad is selling all of Margaret's paintings."

"So?" Sheriff Drake said, handing the newspaper back to me.

"That doesn't strike you as strange?" I said, ignoring the invitation to take the paper back.

"As a matter of fact, no." Realizing I was not about to take the paper, he turned and deposited it in a trash can near his desk.

I took a deep breath and exhaled. I wanted to figure this case out, and it was beginning to feel like I wanted it more than Sheriff Drake. "What about Cathy?" I asked, changing the subject. "Did you find her?"

"No, we haven't," he said, folding his arms in front of his chest and leaning back in his chair. "She could be anywhere by now. It's going to take some time. We'll continue our search in conjunction with police departments around the world. We'll find her. Speaking of traveling, you're free to leave town, but be sure to let this office know how you can be reached."

"You're letting people leave? Are Sandra and Dennis already gone?"

The sheriff looked at his watch. "Well, their plane will be leaving soon."

"What airline and when?"

He shook his head. "That's none of your business. Now, I have a lot of work so if you don't mind leaving." He went back to reviewing the myriad of documents on his desk, but I wasn't about to leave. He slowly looked up and sighed as his eyes met mine. "Mr. Douglas, the door is over there."

"If you aren't going to investigate further, the least you can do is let me. All I want to do is have a final word with them. I might learn something that can crack this case."

Sheriff Drake looked in his desk drawer and pulled out a sheet of paper. "American Airlines, 11:30 AM. You can make it if you leave now."

"You won't regret this," I said, rushing out of his office.

I closed Sheriff Drake's door and walked out toward the front door where Officer Petersen's desk was. "Petersen, just the man I wanted to see." I sat down in the chair in front of his desk and leaned forward. He was still writing so I just stared at him until he gave me his attention.

"Yes?" Petersen said, finally looking up. "What can I do for you?"

"Margaret Wilson case. I can feel it in my bones. The motive was money. Has anyone done a detailed economic background check on the whole family?"

"Yeah," Petersen replied before looking back at his paperwork. "I did."

"Well?" I said, becoming a little frustrated that Petersen was going to make me drag it out of him. "I don't have much time. What did you find out?"

"We subpoenaed financial records. I can't give you specifics, but here's the big picture. Dennis and Sandra are pretty hard up. He rents a small apartment and has only meager savings. Sandra is only a little better off."

"Bottom line is they could really have used some inheritance money?"

"Yeah, but they didn't get anything," Petersen said.

"But, maybe they expected to." Petersen tightened his lips and nodded his head, apparently thinking. "What about James and Cathy?"

"The family has taken care of James pretty well over the years," Petersen said. "He received free housing and a generous wage. Considering his employment, I was surprised how large his savings were. On the other hand, Cathy has very little savings and mounting credit card debt. She's the worst off of everyone."

"Interesting," I said, rubbing my chin. "How about Brad and Rebecca?"

"Well, that was the most surprising. Brad and Rebecca's restaurant has seen a drop in its popularity. The biggest blow came when they got hit with a big lawsuit about six months ago. They pumped more money in the business by almost fully mortgaging their massive estate, but the restaurant hasn't turned around yet."

"Mister Douglas," Sheriff Drake said, walking out of his office with both hands on his hips. "I thought you were going to try to catch a plane."

"I am," I said, rising from my chair. I grabbed a sheet and wrote a quick note. "American Airlines, 11:30, right?" I said, pretending to write that down. Sheriff Drake nodded. I was really writing down something I wanted Petersen to look up. "I was just leaving."

"Good, I'll escort you out then," Sheriff Drake said, walking past me and toward the front of the station. I quickly threw the sheet of paper in front of Petersen. "Just do it please," I whispered to Petersen before turning to follow the sheriff out of the station.

I got in my car and quickly drove to the airport. I parked and raced to the gate arriving in the boarding area at about 11:00 AM. I searched around looking for Dennis and Sandra. I quickly found them sitting next to each other. They were waiting to board the plane.

"Hello," I said to the two, still breathing hard from my run.

"Robert?" Dennis said as both got up from their seats. "What are you doing here?"

"I heard that you two were leaving and I had to talk to you before you left," I said still trying to catch my breath.

"Talk to us?" Sandra asked. "About what?"

"I'm committed to finding out who set that explosive that killed your mother. I just wanted to ask if you remember anything that in retrospect seemed unusual or suspicious."

"We went over this with the police already," Sandra said, sitting back down and folding her arms in front of her chest. "I'm done talking."

"Well, I think the will itself was very suspicious," Dennis said still standing. "For mom to completely exclude Sandra and me, think of all the negative stuff Brad and Rebecca were feeding her."

"I bet both of them knew Brad would get everything too," Sandra said, breaking her short-lived silence. "Maybe they didn't want to wait for mom's death to collect."

"I think Brad's a little bit of a snake, but I can't believe he'd kill mom," Dennis said, looking at Sandra. He then turned and said to me, "But Rebecca, I wouldn't put it past her."

"You think Rebecca would commit murder to receive Margaret's paintings?" I asked. I thought about what Petersen said about the economic struggle of Brad and Rebecca's restaurant. I decided to see what, if anything, Dennis and Sandra knew. "Brad and Rebecca have a successful restaurant business. They aren't hard up for money, are they?"

Sandra and Dennis looked at each other. Then, Sandra folded her arms back across her chest, apparently refusing to address the question. Dennis looked back at me and said, "I wouldn't suppose they would be that hard up, no."

A moment later, an announcement called for boarding on Flight 297. "That's us!" Sandra said as they grabbed their carry-on bags and headed for their gate.

I decided to go back to the Wilsons' estate. I felt if I could just be in the house and reenact everything that happened, I was bound to stumble over a clue to who killed Margaret. As I approached the gate, it opened. Now that was strange. Did someone see me coming? I understood what was going on when a black Mercedes was exiting the estate.

With my car blocking the way, I got out of my car and walked over to the Mercedes. Rebecca was driving with Brad sitting in the passenger's seat. "Would you move your car out of the way?" Rebecca asked as she poked her head out of the window.

"Where are you going?" I asked, bending down to look into the car window. I looked in the backseat and noticed there were several suitcases. "I just wanted to talk to you for a few minutes."

"We have nothing to talk to you about," Rebecca said. "And where we're going is none of your business. Now, would you please move your car?"

"Yeah, sure," I said slowly. "But, I just wanted to tell you how fond of your mother I became. And I'm committed to finding who murdered her."

"Fond of my mother? All you did was take her money!" Brad exclaimed. "Now, get that poor excuse for a car out of the way before I call the police."

I lightly touched the bill of my hat while dipping my head before walking back to my car. After I backed my car up, the Mercedes sped off with the gates immediately closing behind them.

I pulled my car back up to the speaker in front of the closed gate. I certainly wasn't making any friends in the Wilson family, but what bothered me a lot more was that I didn't appear to be getting any closer to solving the case.

"Yes, Mr. Douglas," a voice said with a heavy sigh through the speaker. By now, I easily could recognize James' voice.

"James, please open the gates."

"Mr. and Mrs. Wilson just left. I'm the only one here."

"I know. I want to talk to you."

"Mr. Douglas," James said with another sigh. "I'm very busy."

"I think I can figure out who killed Margaret if you just let me in. Don't you want the person who killed her to be brought to justice?"

There was a long pause. "Drive to the end of the driveway," James said as the gates slowly opened.

I hopped back in my car and slowly drove up the long driveway. I glanced over to right where the greenhouse used to be and shook my head in disgust. James met me outside as I brought my car to a halt. When I got out of my car, he did not lead me back toward the house, which told me that he wanted to conduct our conversation right here.

"I just wanted to ask you," I said, leaning back on the side of the car. "Can you remember anything out of the ordinary that happened that night?"

James thought for a few seconds. "Except for Cathy leaving without telling anyone, no… nothing."

"Ah yes. That certainly doesn't make sense. The police still haven't found her." I thought for a second. "James, do you think Brad or Rebecca killed Margaret?"

"No way. They both loved her." As James looked down at the floor, it appeared as if he might be fighting back emotions. "They loved her a lot. I'd stake my life on it. They didn't set that explosive."

"It just bothers me. Their decision to sell all of those paintings right after her death strikes me as strange."

"It's not strange. They're moving. Why would they want to lug hundreds of paintings with them?"

"Moving? Where are they moving to?"

"Across the country," James replied. They said somewhere in California. They've already left. They took some clothes and stuff, but a moving van will pick the rest up in a couple of days. The house officially goes on sale tomorrow."

"Where does that leave you?"

"Well," James said, scratching behind his ear. "Out of a job." I shook my head, shocked at how many people's lives were changed by Margaret's death. "I can't say that the move surprised me. Brad and Rebecca hired Cathy so I could spend time attending to improving the cosmetics of the estate. I had guessed that they were positioning to sell the home."

"Oh wow. You think the Wilsons were going to move even if Margaret hadn't died?"

"They clearly seemed to be planning for it, but they never said anything." For some reason, I truly trusted James. I still had no idea who the killer was, but I was pretty sure it wasn't him. We tried to reenact the entire day. "You know, this was strange. Brad had to go pick up Margaret's gift, the plants. But, he didn't take his car."

"What car did he take?"

"I don't know," James said thinking. "I just remember that his car, the red Porsche, was still here after he left. I saw it parked on the side."

"I remember you mentioning that. Didn't Rebecca say that he probably took her car?"

"Yeah, but he hates to drive her Mercedes. That's why it's strange."

It was strange. Yet something else that was strange. However, I failed to see how that related in any way to who planted the explosive in the greenhouse. "You give Dennis and Sandra a tour of the estate. Did that include the greenhouse?"

"Yeah, it did. I already told the police this, but I recall Sandra lagged behind a little bit after I showed them the inside of the greenhouse. I didn't think much about it at the time. Because Dennis kept peppering me with so many questions about the estate, I wasn't paying much attention to Sandra."

"Interesting," I said as I planned to switch my focus. "You know, the thing that I can't get over is Cathy abruptly leaving. Do you remember when you caught me snooping around before Sandra and Dennis had arrived?"

"Yes. You had your ear up against the guest bedroom."

"Yeah," I said cracking a smile. "I heard two females arguing. I'm pretty sure it was Cathy and Rebecca. Did they argue a lot?"

"Not really. You know Cathy was new around here. She seemed pretty quiet. It's hard to believe those two would ever get into a heated argument." James continued to go through the day in his mind. After the tour, James said that he went back to preparing dinner. Then, he said that Brad came home and asked him to take the plants out of his car.

"Wait a minute," I said thinking. "Out of which car?"

"His car, the Porsche. And then I brought the plants…"

"Hold on a second. Didn't Brad go to get the plants?" James answered with a nod. "But, I thought you said he didn't take the Porsche."

"He didn't. That car was here after he left. I'm sure of it."

"Then how did the plants that he picked up get into the Porsche which he didn't drive?"

"I don't know," James said.

I drove back to the police station to see if Petersen had gotten any information on my request and to run my theory by him. With the mass exodus of the suspects, the window of opportunity for me to solve this case was rapidly closing.

"Well, did you check on the thing I asked?" I blurted out as soon as I saw Petersen.

"What a greeting. You don't come in here and say, hello, how are you doing? Or am I having a good day?"

"When we solve this case, I'll take you to breakfast and ask all those questions. Right now, I need answers. Did you find out whether Brad and Rebecca had the greenhouse insured?"

"Yeah, I did," Petersen said. "It was fully insured. There was a modest deductible, but they basically didn't lose anything when the greenhouse was blown up." My mouth dropped a bit as my suspicions were confirmed. "There's more. They changed their policy to substantially up their insurance only two months ago."

"I think we just found our killers."

"I don't know," Petersen said, shaking his head. "I think we'll need a little more." I then shared with Petersen my conversation with James which shocked him.

"You have to pick Brad and Rebecca up before they leave town."

"Hold on," Petersen said, grabbing a CB radio. He was trying to reach Sheriff Drake to tell him about the latest information and whether he agreed we had enough to detain Brad and Rebecca. But, there was no response. "He must be away from his car and have his portable CB turned off."

"We need to find out when Brad and Rebecca's flight leaves," I said, trying to get Petersen to refocus.

Petersen sat down at his desk and got on the phone. As I sat down at a nearby chair, I admired Petersen's zeal and commitment. As he talked on the phone, I thought about how I've seen this once rookie officer become a great, senior deputy.

"Thanks, you've been a big help," Petersen said into the phone before hanging up. "Jackpot. They booked three tickets on American flight #310 that leaves at three o'clock. They bought the tickets yesterday."

"Good, we have enough time to…" I said before suddenly stopping. My eyes widened as thoughts raced through my head. My jaw dropped and I instinctively put my left hand up to cover my mouth.

"What's the matter?" Petersen asked confused.

"Three tickets? There's just two of them. Why did they buy three tickets?"

"The butler must be going with them," Petersen offered with a slight shoulder shrug.

"I talked to James earlier today. He's not. So, again I ask, why did they buy three tickets?"

"I don't know. Maybe it was a mistake."

"It was no mistake. Brad and Rebecca bought three tickets for a simple reason. They needed two for them and one for their accomplice."

"Their accomplice?" Petersen repeated with a wrinkled forehead. "Who?"

I looked at my watch. "We have to get to the airport before that flight leaves. I'll explain on the way." I got in the passenger's seat of Petersen's police car. With sirens blaring and lights flashing, we raced to the airport. With confidence, Petersen radioed for back-up help. He was now thoroughly convinced with my theory that Brad and Rebecca were guilty and they had an accomplice.

When we arrived at the airport, Petersen brought the police car to a halt at departures. After getting through security, we looked up at the gate information. "It's gate 7 and it doesn't look like it has boarded yet."

"But it will any minute, come on," I said as we raced to gate 7. "Wait, stop!" I pointed at Brad and Rebecca, who were sitting down near the boarding area of gate 7. "There they are."

"But where's their accomplice?" Petersen asked as we scanned the area.

"I don't know. Should we nab Brad and Rebecca now?"

"No," Petersen said, shaking his head. "We need the accomplice too. Let's lay low until they board. We know where all three of them will be sitting. We'll arrest all of them at that time."

We stayed out of sight until the American Airline flight had fully boarded. Then, Petersen and I walked to the ticketing agent in front of gate 7. Petersen flashed his badge and said, "We have three people on this flight who are suspected of murder. We need to get on this flight and arrest them. This flight can NOT leave until we do this." The flight attendant almost turned ghost white and she nodded repeatedly as she picked up the phone. She called a supervisor and the pilot was then notified that they would not be able to depart until a certain matter with the police was resolved. Finally, almost ten minutes after we had approached the desk at gate 7, several officials led us down the long ramp and onto the plane.

There were a lot of murmurs as we boarded the plane. Apparently, the pilot had told the passengers that there would be a delay. All eyes were on us as we made our way down the aisle of the plane.

When we reached row 9, Brad and Rebecca sat in their seats with disturbed looks on their faces. When Petersen and I came to a stop at their row, Brad asked, "What's going on here?"

I looked over to seat C, the seat that should have contained Brad and Rebecca's accomplice, but it clearly didn't. Sitting in seat C was a guy in his early 20s. The guy wore a tie dyed shirt and blue jeans. My heart beat quickened as I momentarily wondered if I was wrong. I looked at Petersen who still seemed to be keeping his poise.

"Sir," Petersen said to the guy in the tie dyed shirt. "Do you know either of these two people?" Petersen asked, pointing to Brad and Rebecca.

"Nah," the man said, shaking his head. I could see Petersen close his eyes slightly which was a little sign of his frustration with the recent turn of events.

"What's going on here?" Brad asked again.

"That's a good question!" a voice boomed from the front of the plane. It was Sheriff Drake. "Care to explain deputy?"

All of a sudden, Deputy Petersen was on the hot seat. Everyone on the plane looked at him while my mind continued to race to make sense of all this.

"I was about to make an arrest," Petersen said softly to Sheriff Drake. "We have evidence that Brad and Rebecca set the explosive to go off in their greenhouse."

"What?" Brad said, jumping out of his scat. "This is ridiculous. I loved my mother. I would never have killed her."

"Wait a minute," Petersen said, sticking his index finger in the air. "I didn't say you killed your mother. I only said that you set the explosive."

"Isn't that the same thing?" Sheriff Drake asked.

"Well, no," Petersen said slowly. "You see, I called the airline and they indicated that Brad had purchased three tickets on his credit card."

"Is that what this is about?" Brad asked. "It was some mix-up when I ordered it over the phone."

"Excuse me," a representative from the airline said. "We need to get this plane airborne. You need to either make an arrest or off-board the plane."

Sheriff Drake turned to Petersen. "I haven't heard anything that justifies arresting either of these…"

"Hold it," I said as I looked directly at the man in the tie dyed shirt. "You are currently in 9C. Is that the seat you had booked when you boarded this plane?"

"Nah, it's not," the man said as Brad and Rebecca closed their eyes in frustration. "A nice lady asked if I would switch with her. She had a window and I had a middle seat so I said sure."

"What was your original seat sir?" Petersen asked.

"16B," the man said. Petersen immediately headed further down the aisle with Sheriff Drake and me right behind him. Seated in 16B was a woman heavily covered in makeup with a large bandana covering her head. "Sheriff," Petersen said with a slight smile. "Let me introduce you to Brad and Rebecca's accomplice in murder." Petersen asked the woman to remove her scarf. Even though she had a lot of makeup on, the woman was clearly Margaret Wilson.

"It can't be," Sheriff Drake said. "If this is Margaret, then whose remains did we find after the explosion?"

"Let me put it to you this way sheriff," I said, putting my hand on his shoulder. "I think you can call off that worldwide search for Cathy. You already found her."

Margaret, Brad, and Rebecca were taken off the plane and down to the police station. We were in Sheriff Drake's office when he asked, "Do you three have any statements to make?"

"We're not saying anything until our lawyer gets here," Rebecca said.

"You don't have to speak, but you will listen," Sheriff Drake said before turning to Petersen. "How did you figure it out?"

"I got some help from Robert," Petersen said as he gestured toward me. "I'll let him tell it."

"Okay," I said, trying to decide where to begin. "There were a lot of things that didn't make sense about that day. But the biggest mystery was why Cathy left without telling anyone, when she was supposed to work the entire night. When James told me that Brad didn't take his Porsche to pick up the plants for Margaret's birthday, I wasn't suspicious. However, when James later remembered that he took the plants out of the Porsche, I knew something was strange. I then was able to put two and two together. Rebecca had left to pick up Margaret's birthday cake. She must have taken Brad's Porsche while Brad drove Cathy's car to the airport making it look like she skipped town. Rebecca must have followed Brad to the airport and transported him and the plants back to the house.

Margaret simply stared at the floor. I couldn't understand how she could take part in a murder. She really fooled me. Looking back, I now understand why she acted so strange all the time. Why she seemed more intrigued than scared. Why should she ever have been afraid? She knew her life was never in danger.

"Now when Margaret went into the greenhouse about five minutes elapsed before the explosion occurred," I said. "That was plenty of time for her to slip out the back way. The back of the greenhouse faced the gates. So, she could run out of the gates without being noticed."

Shaking his head in disgust, Sheriff Drake then blurted out, "But she left Cathy in the greenhouse to be blown up." The sheriff thanked me for my assistance, but said that it was time for me to leave.

I didn't argue. My mission was complete.

The next morning I was enjoying breakfast in a nearby, almost empty diner. Sitting across from me in the booth in the corner of the diner was Deputy Petersen. He leaned over closer to me and said in a lower tone, "So Rebecca finally came clean once her lawyer arrived. It turned out that she, Brad and Margaret had an elaborate plan. You see, they were in financial peril."

"Well, we knew their restaurant was struggling and they had to mortgage their home to the hilt, but financial peril?"

"For their lifestyle, yeah," Petersen replied before raising his hand to catch the waitresses' attention. The waitress came over and we both ordered coffee and the breakfast special. Once the waitress left, Petersen looked back at me. "Where was I? Oh yeah, they were really desperate financially. Creditors were becoming more aggressive. To meet their obligations, they knew the restaurant and their home would have to be sold to pay off all their debts."

"Ah... but they wouldn't have a home or anything to live on."

"That's right," Peterson said. "Margaret actually suggested this scheme of faking her death so they could net over half a million dollars on the sale of her paintings. That's a nice nest egg. With their restaurant and home sold, they were free to move to California where no one would ever recognize Margaret. She didn't know many people..." Petersen abruptly stopped as the waitress placed two cups of coffee down at our table before quickly departing.

"What a wild idea," I said, shaking my head. "But why did they get me involved in this hoax?"

"They wanted to raise the suspicion that she was actually murdered. It really skyrocketed the price of the paintings. Plus, you would add more validity that she really did die." Petersen stirred additional cream into his cup of coffee before saying, "They really only made one mistake."

"And what's that?"

"They let Cathy overhear one of their conversations discussing this scheme. Cathy confronted Rebecca and threatened to expose their little plan if they didn't buy her off."

"Oh my gosh!" I said, lightly smacking myself on the forehead. "I think I overheard that. At the time, I didn't really understand what it all meant."

"Well, what it meant was the death of Cathy," Petersen said. "Cathy and Rebecca's conversation became very heated. Rebecca claims that Cathy even physically threatened her and Rebecca responded, in a moment of rage, smacking Cathy in the temple with some type of trophy that was in the room." My jaw instinctively dropped in surprise. "Rebecca claims that there was never any intention to kill her."

"But she did. And then they decided to take advantage of the fact that they had a dead body."

"Yeah, they figured that they could kill two birds with one stone," Petersen said, taking a sip of his coffee. "They easily disposed of Cathy's body in the greenhouse. They knew any indistinguishable remains would be assumed to be Margaret's, bolstering the murder theory."

At that moment, the waitress returned with our breakfast specials. I enjoyed a relaxed breakfast no longer haunted by the words "someone is trying to kill me."

"Sheriff Drake was really impressed with my work on this case," Petersen said as the waitress dropped off the check. "I guess I owe you a debt of gratitude for your help."

"Well, I owe you something as well." I pulled out my credit card and cleared my throat before saying, "How are you? Are you having a good day?"

Petersen laughed, remembering our earlier conversation. "I'm having a great day. Thanks for asking."

The Death Of Seth

I took a deep breath before looking up to see
A scared, frightened woman looking back at me.

Her entire body seemed to tremble in sheer fright
as I thought about the tragic events that took place this night.

"Get a hold of yourself," I muttered in anger.
But, I felt like I was looking at a stranger.

I didn't recognize the woman with the bruises all over her face.
I didn't know the woman who would often cry in disgrace.

It was the physical and mental abuse that made her this way
And it drove her to shoot her husband this day.

Using a loud shotgun sure wasn't smart,
But it wasn't premeditated to put a bullet in his heart.

The husband Seth was drunk and in a bad mood
Outraged that, awaiting him, was no hot food.

Seth pounded unmercifully as if he was actually having fun
Until he knocked her next to the family's shotgun.

It's easy to criticize, second guess, and even finger point,
But after the many beatings, everyone has their breaking point.

I always thought the fear would go away if Seth would just die
But I didn't foresee the fear of prosecution and I started to cry.

"I'll find a way out of this," I said to the woman in front of me.
"Everything is going to work out, you'll see."

Tears rolled down her bruised face as I quickly wiped them
away.
"Open the front door! It's the police!" I heard a man's voice say.

I peered out from the upstairs bathroom to sneak a glance
As the police, who saw Seth's body, warned of a last chance.

I heard the windows shatter as the police broke in, showing no
fear.
Announcing their arrival, they yelled if there was anyone here.

I stayed upstairs standing in complete silence,
while the police readied themselves for possible violence.

I looked back at the woman's bruised face and thought of the
many years of denial.
But then a strange thing happened. The woman began to smile.

I winked at the woman and she winked back.
I realized there was now evidence for why there was an attack.

The bruises show self-defense was the motive for the killing.
"I'll survive this thing," I said. "God willing."

The Death of Seth

I took a deep breath and the woman did the same
And an overwhelming feeling of peace suddenly came.

I then heard the sounds of police footsteps as they came nearer
And I continued to look at the woman in the mirror.

For once, as I looked in the mirror, I was proud to see
that the badly beaten, but determined woman was me.

When the Personals Get Personal

Young, humorous, attractive woman seeking SWM who I met on the subway that arrived in San Francisco on the morning of September 25th. You are about six feet tall and stunningly handsome. You mentioned that you loved running, sports and the great outdoors. We shared a joke together about another passenger. You gave me your business card, but I misplaced it. Please send an email to address below so we can reunite.

Karen stared at her ad in the morning paper and let out a noticeable sigh. Three days the ad had run and the only responses that she had received over the email were from a few sickos and practical joke artists. Karen remembered the man's name and title on the business card: Ryan the Marketing Manager. "Model-like looks and money. I think I'm in love," Karen thought to herself.

"Has he responded yet?" Allison asked, entering Karen's room. Allison was Karen's friend and roommate. Just a week ago, Allison helped her roommate turn their two-bedroom apartment upside-down to unsuccessfully look for the Ryan's business card.

"Not yet," Karen said, folding up the newspaper. She did not exaggerate with her ad. An attractive woman, Karen had beautiful blond hair that seductively dropped to her shoulders and surrounded her pretty face.

"When was the last time you checked your email?" Allison asked.

"I just checked an hour ago."

"Well, maybe something has come in since then." Allison reached over Karen to grab the mouse. As Allison clicked to the proper website, Karen strained her neck to look over Allison's shoulder. "You got a new message!" Allison said, causing Karen to jump up to look at the screen.

> I saw your ad today in the paper and it made my day. I wondered why you had not called me. I would greatly like to treat you to dinner at Luigi's restaurant in San Francisco. I hope you will meet me this Friday night promptly at 7:00 PM. I will have a table reserved.
>
> I remember our conversation on the subway that morning vividly. We discussed my wish to run every morning at 6:00 AM and that my favorite sports team is the NY Yankees. If I remember correctly, your name is Karen.
>
> -Ryan

When the letter referenced his running habits and favorite sports team, she knew this was it. The final confirmation was the last two words of the letter. When she saw her name and then Ryan's name, Karen jumped up and celebrated because neither name was mentioned in her personal ad.

Karen had spent almost two hours Friday afternoon getting ready for her big date. Already a beautiful woman, Karen's visit to the hair salon and manicure made her the walking personification of gorgeous.

"Ryan will be blown away," Allison said with a gasp as she clasped Karen's hand in a supporting gesture.

"Thanks," Karen said before pulling her hand away to admire herself in the mirror. Then, she looked down at her watch. "I better go. The email said to be there at exactly seven o'clock."

Karen took a step toward the front door when Allison grabbed a hold of her hand again. "I've been thinking about this meeting. This could be dangerous. Remember all of the other emails you got. There were some real sickos."

"There's nothing to worry about," Karen said. "I'm sure this response is from Ryan."

"What if *Ryan* is a sicko?"

Karen automatically shook her head in disagreement. "Ryan's no sicko. He's a great guy. And he's crazy about me."

"Or just plain crazy," Allison mumbled to herself. "I'm sorry to bring this up at the last minute. I just have a bad feeling about this. Maybe I should go with…"

"No! I need to do this alone." There was a short, uncomfortable pause as the two women stared at each other. "What could possibly go wrong? I'll be in a restaurant with hundreds of other people."

Allison walked over to her purse and dug her hands into it. "Okay, but to be on the safe side," Allison said, pulling out a small spray can in her hand. Karen's forehead wrinkled as she stared at the spray can. "It's mace."

Karen shook her head. "I really don't need…"

"Just take it. You can keep it in your purse. In case anything goes wrong, spray it directly into his eyes. And one more thing, watch his hands at all times. Make sure he doesn't slip anything in your drink or in your food."

"Okay, okay, may I go now?" Karen said, rolling her eyes as she put the spray in her purse. Allison stepped to the side and gestured toward the door with an open hand. "Thank you," Karen said before taking a deep breath. Now she had a feeling of fear to be mixed in with excitement and nervousness. The pit of her stomach turned as she walked out of her apartment bound for Luigi's.

Karen arrived at Luigi's ten minutes early. She waited in her car in the parking lot for about seven minutes so that she could enter the restaurant exactly on time as the email requested. While she waited, she admired herself in the mirror and made sure her make-up was perfectly in place. It relaxed her to see how beautiful she was. She had a renewed confidence that everything would be okay.

She walked with confidence toward the restaurant. When Karen entered Luigi's, the maitre d' notified her that her party was waiting for her. She couldn't help but smile knowing that Ryan was not a "no show."

"Right this way ma'am," the maitre d' said, leading Karen into the elegant dining area. As she was led through a labyrinth of tables, Karen witnessed a sea of romantic, candle-lit place settings and smelled the aroma of fresh cooked pasta sauces and spices. She impatiently looked forward, hoping to get a glimpse of Ryan.

Karen almost ran into the maitre d' as he suddenly stopped at a table. "Your table ma'am," the maitre d' said, lifting his left hand toward a small table where a complete stranger sat. Her heart sank as an overwhelming sense of disappointment swarmed her body.

"There appears to be a mistake," Karen muttered to the maitre d' before looking back at the pudgy, spectacled man at the table. Karen again scanned the restaurant looking for Ryan.

"No mistake," the pudgy man said. "Ryan will be here any minute." With the word "Ryan", a chill shot through Karen and she stopped searching the restaurant and refocused her attention on the pudgy man. "I'm a close friend of his." He motioned with his hand. "Please, Karen, have a seat."

Another chill went directly up Karen's spine. He knew her name. There was an uncomfortable pause as Karen looked at the maitre d' and back at the pudgy man. "Okay," she said before taking a seat.

"Could you please tell our waiter to bring out another bottle of Cabernet Sauvignon?" the pudgy man asked. The maitre d' nodded before leaving the table.

Karen wondered what was going on. She reached into her purse and felt for the can of mace to make sure it was there. It was. She noticed that her heartbeat quickened as she waited for him to talk. She focused in on his hands, which rested on the table. He introduced himself, but Karen did not quite catch the name. She didn't bother to ask him to repeat it. She couldn't imagine why it would ever be important. All that was important was the whereabouts of Ryan.

"You're probably wondering what's going on here," the pudgy man said with an uneasy smile. Karen answered the rhetorical question with a nod. "Ryan asked me to meet with you and talk to you for a few minutes. Just to make sure you're not a psycho or anything." He laughed awkwardly as Karen remained silent. She took her hands off the mace inside her purse and sat up in her chair a bit as the realization that this was some kind of interview. "Look, we'll talk for a few moments. After I ask you just a few questions, I'll call Ryan on his cell phone and he'll be here in less than five minutes. Then, you two can be alone for the rest of the evening."

"Okay," Karen said, not clear what choice she really had. The two talked openly for a couple of minutes. He asked Karen about her profession, her hobbies, and her family. A bottle of wine was delivered to the table. The waiter opened the bottle at the table and filled each of their glasses.

"I'd like to propose a toast," the pudgy man said with a smile. "Here's to taking risks to find happiness." Karen, still feeling uncomfortable, nodded tentatively. The two clanked glasses together. Karen put the glass up to her nose and cautiously waited until he drank before she did the same. He pointed to a small menu sitting on the table. "Go ahead and order an appetizer. Ryan is going to be picking up the tab."

Karen scanned the menu for a moment. "I think I'll have a salad. How about you?"

"Oh, I'm not hungry," he replied before flagging down the waiter to put in Karen's order. He then started to talk about how this was his favorite wine. Karen currently was at the table only in body. Her mind was elsewhere, thinking about Ryan. Why would he really pull this stunt with the pudgy man? Was it really some kind of test? Was this some kind of joke? Karen thought about her personal ad and looked back at the man with whom she was sharing a table. "When I said I was seeking a SWM, I didn't mean short, wide male," Karen snickered to herself. She wished that Ryan were here to enjoy her joke.

"Karen!" the pudgy man said, waving his hand. "Are you listening to me?"

"Of course I am."

"Ryan specifically asked me to ask you this question." He paused to clear his throat, capturing Karen's interest for the first time. "Do you believe in love at first sight?"

"Of course I do," Karen said. "I fell in love with Ryan on that subway train." She sat back in her chair and gestured with her right hand while saying, "Why else would I take out an ad to try to find him? So, do you know if Ryan believes in love at first sight?"

"Well, I don't know how Ryan feels, but I think it's an impossible phenomenon."

"How come?" Karen asked, actually showing interest in something the pudgy man had to say.

"By definition, love at first sight means you feel some strong emotion without knowing anything about the person." He paused to finish his glass of wine. "You can't love someone solely based on how they appear on the outside. You love someone for what's on the inside and that's impossible to determine at first sight."

"Sounds like fortune cookie logic to me." There was another uncomfortable pause in the conversation, as the pudgy man appeared disappointed at Karen's response.

The waiter broke the awkward silence. "Here you are ma'am, the house salad. Would you like pepper on your salad?"

Karen nodded and the waiter slowly dispensed the pepper. While this was happening, the pudgy man said, "My friend and I would like some bread."

"Yes, of course," the waiter said before scurrying away.

"Look, you seem pretty sane to me. And I know you didn't come here to talk to me." He paused to see if Karen would bite at his fish for a compliment. She remained silent as he realized her mind was someplace else again. "I'm going to call Ryan from the pay phone and have him come right over."

Karen smiled broadly at the remark and seemed to breathe a small sigh of relief. The pudgy man got up from the table and walked back toward the front of the restaurant where she remembered the pay phones were located. Karen felt awkward being alone at the table. She poured herself more wine. As she took a sip, she looked around at the tables nearby, almost all containing romantic couples. "Gosh, I hope no one thought I was on a date with him." Karen laughed at the thought of it as she began to eat her salad.

The man paused at the front of the restaurant. He surveyed the two unused pay phones in the corner. He took off his glasses, which he rarely ever wore, and put them in his coat before walking away from the pay phones and out of the restaurant. The man waved his hand to flag down an approaching cab.

The man never contacted Ryan. He did not even know Ryan as he had claimed. In fact, the only time that he had seen Ryan was on a morning subway train that was bound for San Francisco. That morning, he sat across from Karen and Ryan who loudly flirted with each other. And when he got up from his seat, he distinctly heard the couple make a joke about his weight, which was followed by stifled laughter. The man wished they could be taught a lesson.

As the man got into the cab, he smiled at having gotten his revenge, while enjoying $200 worth of fine food and wine, for which Karen would soon be asked to pay.

The Confession

A young priest in mind, body, and spirit, Father John Flockhart helped members of the community, one person at a time. Whether young or old, rich or poor, sick or healthy, John strove to make their lives a little better and a little more meaningful. He believed in *doing* God's work. He didn't just pray for change in his community, he made change.

This Saturday afternoon, he conducted confessionals. Because of his compassion and vibrant personality, he earned the trust of many of his parishioners. He settled in his chair and awaited the first confession of the day.

Father John heard someone enter, opened the slit of the confessional and immediately recognized the man. It was Sam Weston. Arrested for shoplifting as a teenager, Sam met Father John when he completed his community service sentence. He took Sam under his wing and helped turn his life around. A brilliant young mind, Sam scored a perfect 800 on his math SAT. He went on to college, earning a Bachelor's degree in accounting. He had a good job and owned a home in the neighborhood.

"Forgive me Father, for I have sinned," Sam said, his hands trembling as he suddenly felt claustrophobic in the small confessional. "I've had trouble sleeping and have lost my appetite."

"What is the nature of your sin?" John asked.

A lump formed in Sam's throat. "You know how I run the accounting department at my job. Well, they rent apartments, and about three months ago, I borrowed some money from the company."

"Borrowed or stole?"

"No, borrowed. I have every intention of giving it back. I receive some rents checks every month for almost a thousand apartment units. For one month, I signed nearly half the rent checks to my personal account. To cover the deficiency on the books, I applied the following month's check to each account."

"Um, Sam?" John said. He tilted his head slightly. "That's stealing. How much did you take?"

Sam dropped his head, pausing for a moment. "About $400,000."

"What did you do with the money?"

"I used it to buy some stock. It was a can't-miss investment, a once in a life time opportunity. I was going to return the money within four months."

John frowned. "I'm guessing that the stock went bad."

"No, it has gone through the roof. I doubled the money. The problem is that I cannot get my hands on the money for another two months. The owner of the company has been acting strange lately. I can tell he's suspicious. I'm worried he'll find out before I can return the money."

"You need to tell the owner what you've done. Let him know you will return all of the money in two months, with interest."

"I can't do that," Sam said, shaking his head. "He could tell the police. I could go to jail, for a long time. I can't risk that."

John leaned forward. "If you are not willing to face the consequences of your actions, you aren't really asking for forgiveness." There was silence. "Sam?"

"Yes," Sam said, snapping out of his many random thoughts. "Okay, I'll tell him by the end of the day on Monday."

"Good. He'll appreciate your honesty."

"Yes, I do owe him that. He has been really good to me. Okay, is there anything else I should do?"

"There is one thing," John said. "Do you think that you should profit from your sin?"

Sam stared at John for a moment before sighing. "Whatever doesn't go back to my company will go to charity."

John smiled. "Very good."

It had been over two hours of confessional after confessional when a close friend entered. John opened the slit. It was Carl Jacobson. They had become close friends, even though Carl was almost thirty years his senior. A successful businessman, Carl believed in giving back to the community.

"Oh Father John, I really screwed up. Real bad," Carl said, with fear in his eyes.

John was stunned. Usually calm and composed, Carl seemed to be on the verge of a nervous breakdown. "Try to calm down and just tell me what you've done."

"You won't tell anyone about anything I say here?"

"No, I won't. Anything you tell me is completely private. What have you done, Carl?"

"You know I've been thinking of selling my business and retiring. Well, I received an excellent offer from a buyer. Normally, I never look at the books too closely. But, as a part of the sale, the buyer's accountants audited the books. They determined without a doubt that my accounting manager Sam, the kid you recommended I hire, had embezzled $400,000. The buyer called off the deal."

"Did you confront Sam and ask him about it?"

"No, that's not how I handled it. I was very upset and a little drunk."

John squinted and asked slowly, "What did you do?"

"After I found out the deal was blown, I went out Saturday night to hit the bars. I happened to meet up with an acquaintance and I told him the whole story. He said that Sam should pay the ultimate price for his betrayal and he knew how to make it happen. And I, uh, agreed to it."

"Are you saying you hired a hitman to kill Sam?" John asked. Carl nodded slowly. John's voice cracked as he said, "Are you crazy?"

"I know, I know. It was stupidest thing I've ever done in my entire life. I was tired, drunk, and still really mad at what Sam did. I wasn't thinking straight. But, it hasn't happen yet. It's supposed to happen Monday, two days from now."

"Well, call it off."

"That's the problem. I've been trying. Charlie, my acquaintance, is just the middle man. He gets the hitman, but I'm never told who he is. It protects both parties."

"Then contact Charlie and have him call it off."

"That's what I've been trying to do," Carl said with exasperation. "I originally talked to Charlie six days ago, in the wee hours of the morning on Sunday. But I realized what a terrible mistake I made the very next morning and contacted Charlie to call it off. I couldn't get ahold of him on Monday, Tuesday, Wednesday, or Thursday. On Friday, I found out."

"What? What did you find out?"

"Charlie died in a car crash late Sunday night. Father, I'm very worried. Charlie may have already arranged the hit." John fell back in his chair, stunned. "If he did arrange the hit, I know it's going to happen this Monday at 5:00 PM at my office."

"Wait a minute," John said. "You don't know who the hitman is, but you know when and where?"

"Yes, that's part of the deal. After I paid Charlie, he told me when and where, so I could be far away with other people. You know, so I have an alibi."

John paused a minute. "Carl, you have to go to the police."

The Confession

"I can't do that. I'll go to jail for the rest of my life. But, if I can just stop it from happening, then no one ever has to know."

"How can you stop it? You have no way of getting in touch with the hitman."

"No, but I know he's going to be at my office at 5:00 PM. I can tell him that I'm calling it off. He can keep the money."

John leaned forward. "That can be dangerous."

"I don't care. I have to make this right."

John thought for a moment. "I understand that, but this is important. Sam can't be anywhere near your office at five o'clock."

"I need him there," Carl said.

"That's out of the question," John said, shaking his head. "You shouldn't put his life in danger."

"His life already is in danger. If Sam is not there, the hitman might not come. Then, we won't have any idea when and where the hit will occur. There will be no way to stop it."

Father John buried his face in his hands. The charismatic, talkative priest was at a loss for words.

It was four o'clock on Monday afternoon. Father John felt a faint breeze as he stood outside of Carl's one story office building. Dressed in black slacks and a black shirt with a white collar, John held a duffle bag. He opened the glass front door and walked inside. In the first room, he was greeted by the receptionist.

"Hello there. Welcome to Sierra Heights," the woman said. The woman, who appeared to be in her sixties, had a smile that lit up the room. "How can I help you?" she asked as John made it to the reception desk.

John smiled back at the cheerful woman. "Is Carl in?"

"Yes, he is. Your name, sir." John told her, and the woman, who wore a phone headset, dialed Carl's extension. "Hi, John is here to see you." The woman then said to John, "He'll be right out."

As John waited, he looked outside to see if he could spot anyone suspicious. The street was pretty empty. There were a couple of parked cars, but he didn't see anyone.

"Father John," Carl said. The priest turned around and the two men shook hands. "Let's go to my office." Carl led John back to his office and the two sat down. "I really appreciate you coming down. I'm a nervous wreck."

"Well, try to calm yourself," John said. "Who's in the building now?"

"Just us, Sam, and the receptionist, Ellen. I sent everyone else home."

"You should send Ellen home too, so she's not here when the hitman arrives."

"Oh, don't worry. I already told her that she needs to leave early. I just need her to handle the phones and greet anyone up until then." Carl and Sam went over their plan.

"Remember our agreement. Sam stays locked in his office the entire time," John said. Carl nodded in response. "I need to talk to him. Where's his office?"

"Further down the hall, third office on the left," Carl said, pointing.

John walked down the hallway, stopping at the office with the name plate "Sam Weston." For a few seconds, John observed Sam typing on his computer keyboard. He knocked on the open door to get his attention.

"Father John! What a surprise," Sam said, straightening his tie. John closed the door behind him. John noticed that the office did not have any windows. "I haven't talked to Carl yet about what I did," Sam whispered. "But, I will. I promise. I kind of wanted to do it at the very end of the day."

"Do you trust me?" John asked abruptly.

Sam's forehead wrinkled. "Of course."

"Are you expecting any calls or visitors for the next hour and a half?" Sam shook his head. "Great," John said, reaching into his duffle bag and pulling out a bulletproof vest. "Put this under your sweater."

Sam took the vest, clearly perplexed. "Why? What's going on?"

"I can't go into details. Besides, the less you know, the better."

"What are you talking about?" The tie around Sam's neck felt like a noose and he momentarily found it difficult to breathe. "I want to know. What's going on?"

"You told me that you trusted me, right?" Sam nodded. "Then, just put this vest on."

After Sam put the vest on, John led him further down the hall to another internal office. "I want you to stay here for the next hour and a half. Keep the door locked. Don't open the door unless you hear my voice, requesting it. Got it?"

"Yeah," Sam said, his heart racing.

John walked back toward the hallway, pausing at the doorway. "Please stay in here, okay?"

John started to close the door, but Sam caught it with his hand. "You're really starting to scare me. How worried should I be?"

John stared at him for a moment. "Just do exactly as I described." John closed the door and waited until he heard the door being locked from the inside.

John walked back to Carl's office. The two men rehearsed how they would handle the conversation with the hitman. It was 4:50 when the office phone rang.

"Yes Ellen," Carl said, answering on his speaker phone.

"You asked me to direct any visitors for Sam to you," Ellen said. "There's a Steven Raynolds here to see Sam. He says he has an appointment."

Carl looked at John. A chill went up John's spine.

"Okay, I'll be right out," Carl said into the phone.

After Carl ended the phone call, John immediately said, "I talked to Sam. He told me that he didn't have any appointments on his schedule."

"This must be our guy then," Carl said, rising. "Let's go."

As the two men walked toward the lobby, John said, "You need to get Ellen out of here now."

When they arrived in the lobby, they spotted a middle aged man wearing a sports jacket over slacks and a dress shirt. Clean shaven with a sturdy build, he had a serious expression on his face.

"Steven Raynolds?" Carl said, shaking the man's hand. "I'm Carl, Sam's boss. Sam is wrapping up a meeting. He'll be right out." Carl gestured toward a glass-windowed conference room behind the receptionist. "Please, you can wait in there."

Steven walked into the conference room, while Carl quickly said to Ellen, "I'd like you to pack up and go home."

"But it's not five thirty yet," Ellen said, appearing confused.

"That's okay," Carl said. "I want you to go home early. So, please pack up right now."

"Okay," Ellen said, slowly. She gathered her belongings as Carl and John watched. "Well, have a good night," she said before walking out the front door.

Carl walked over to the front door and locked it. He felt comforted to watch her safely walk away.

"So, you ready?" John asked.

Carl turned around. "Ready as I'll ever be." Both men walked toward the conference room.

Carl and John sat down at the conference room table across from Steven. "There is something that I need to say to you,"

Carl said to Steven. "I need you to listen very carefully. You don't need to say anything."

Steven's forehead wrinkled. "Uh, okay."

Carl nervously rubbed his face before saying, "I believe we have a mutual friend. His name is Charlie Mansino. I asked Charlie to do something. In turn, he may have asked you to do something. But, there has been a change of plans. It's off. I don't want you to do it anymore." Carl dipped his head. "Understand?"

Steven squinted, then glanced back and forth between Carl and John. "No, I don't. I don't know what you're talking about."

"Look, I'm serious. It's off. You don't have to do it. If you got any money, keep it. I just want you to leave and never come back."

Steven flashed a perplexed look. "This is weird. I just want to see Sam."

"You can't see him," Carl said. "He's not here."

Steven looked at the tight-lipped John and then back at Carl. "You're lying. He's here. I know it."

Carl rose from his chair. "The only thing that you need to know is, it is off. Now, I think you should leave."

Steven stood up as well. "Just take me to Sam."

"No," Carl said, shaking his head. "I'm not going to do that."

"I think that you will," Steven said, reaching inside his sports jacket to pull out a handgun. "Take me to him now."

John slowly rose. "You're going to have to shoot us because we aren't taking you to Sam. I suggest you leave now and we can forget this whole meeting took place."

Steven paused as if he were contemplating his options. At that moment, Ellen unlocked the front door and walked over to the reception desk. Steven slipped out of the conference room and, pointing the gun at Ellen, said, "Freeze!"

A startled Ellen let out a short scream. "I just forgot my show tickets. I left them in my desk drawer."

"Get in the conference room," Steven said.

Ellen briskly walked into the conference room. "What's going on?" she asked with a frantic tone. Carl remained silent, angered that he had now involved Ellen in this.

"I'm looking for Sam," Steven said. "If someone can take me to him, no one will get hurt."

"He's in his office, just down the hallway," Ellen said.

"Thank you. Was that so tough?" Steven grabbed ahold of Ellen. "Okay, we're going to get Sam. If anyone tries anything, this nice lady is going to pay the price." John and Carl looked at each other, feeling powerless.

Ellen led Steven to Sam's office, followed by Carl and John. They opened Sam's office, and it was empty.

"I told you he wasn't here," Carl said.

"We're checking every one of these offices," Steven said. One by one, the caravan opened the offices and searched them to no avail. "This office is locked," Steven said, jiggling the handle. He looked at Carl. "You must have a master key."

Carl paused to ponder his options until Steven put the handgun to Ellen's head. "Unlock the door."

Carl reached for the key in his pocket and unlocked the door. "Get out of the way," Steven said, pushing Carl to the side while still dragging Ellen as a hostage. "Sam, you in here?" Steven asked to the apparently empty room.

Sam slowly rose from the behind the desk and said, "Thank goodness it's you. What are you doing with a gun?"

"These guys gave me the run-around," Steven said, gesturing to the others.

Stunned, John asked, "What's going on?"

"Put the gun away," Sam said. "These people are my friends. And let go of Ellen. She's our receptionist, for gosh sakes."

164

When Steven let go of Ellen, she collapsed on the floor.

"Oh my gosh, someone get her some water," Sam said.

Carl raced out of the room while Sam and John helped Ellen up onto a chair. John lightly patted her face, trying to bring her around. "You know this man?" John asked Sam.

"Yes, Steven's a friend. I've known him for many years. When you gave me a bullet proof vest, I was concerned. He's a former Marine. I called him here to protect me."

"Well, he's crazy. He put a gun to her head."

"That's because no one would tell me where Sam was," Steven said, standing in the corner, his handgun tucked safely away. "I wasn't going to hurt her."

Carl returned with a cup of water. John dabbed a little on Ellen's face and she began to come around and even took a small sip.

John looked at his watch and pulled Carl over to the side. He whispered, "It's 5:26 PM. The hitman was supposed to be here at five o'clock, but no one came. It looks like Charlie died before he ever made contact with the hitman."

"Yes, it's over," Carl said, exhaling audibly. "But look what happened to Ellen. I'm ultimately responsible."

"Does she have any history of medical problems?" John asked Carl.

"I don't know. She's only been here a couple of days. She's a temp. My regular receptionist is out on disability."

"Oh," John said as he watched Ellen slowly sitting up in her chair.

"I think I'm okay," Ellen said.

"Alright," Sam said, turning his attention from Ellen to John. "I want to know what's going on here. I have been locked in this office for the last hour thinking my life was in danger."

"It was all a big misunderstanding," Carl said. "We're sorry."

"A misunderstanding?" Sam said, eyes widened in disbelief. "Put on a bullet proof vest because someone might kill you is not a misunderstanding. You scared me half to death! What made you think my life was in danger?"

"Sam. Sit down and relax, okay," John said.

As if against his will, Sam slowly sat down and Ellen offered him some of her water. "No thanks," Sam said, still upset.

"Take it," Ellen insisted.

John's mind was working fast. Sam took the cup from Ellen and John shouted, "Stop! Don't drink that. Put that cup down." John had startled everyone in the room, including Steven, who reflexively drew his gun.

Sam slowly put the cup down on the table. John walked over and took the cup. "There's nothing wrong with that water. I just drank from it," Ellen said.

"You're right. There was nothing wrong with it when *you* drank from it," John said.

Ellen squinted as she tilted her head. "Are you accusing me of putting something in that cup?"

John ignored Ellen's question and instead turned toward Carl. "You said that Ellen has been working at a temp for just two days. When did you first learn she would be working here?" John raised his eyebrows. "Was it within the last week, since you had your conversation with Charlie?"

Carl's eyes widened. "Yes, it was."

John looked at Ellen. "We can have this water tested, but we both know what we would find. Now, listen closely. Originally, we contacted Charlie Mansino. We're calling it off and that's the last we speak of this. Do you understand?"

Ellen slowly nodded her head. John looked at Carl and said, "Now, it's over."

About the Stories

WARNING: This section should not be read until AFTER you have read all of the stories in this book. In this section, I do give away some of the clues, climax, and conclusion of the stories.

I think I was sitting in a college English class once and the instructor asked us to analyze and interpret a particular story. A student mumbled some gibberish about the story being a "commentary on man's struggle against forces out of his control" and I swear I could feel the ground move slightly from the author turning over in his grave. It sure would be nice if the author wrote a section explaining what the story was "really" about.

That said, even hearing from the author does not mean that is the "right" answer. An author's craft is similar to a painter's. When a painter completes his or her artwork, what a person "sees" in the painting is just as important as what the author may have intended. And I believe that is the beauty of art. One person can see something completely different from another. However, that does not mean one viewpoint is necessarily more "right" than another. It's just different.

Here are some of my thoughts about the stories in this book. It might enlighten you to a different perspective and view of the stories that you have recently read. Enjoy…

When My World Got Turned Upside Down

My mother always told me, "Write about what you know." I can sympathize all too well with the narrator's predicament of working late at the opening of the story. In fact, on many occasions in real life, I have called my home to leave a reminder message to do something. Several times I have asked myself, "What if someone answered?" And the beginning of the idea to write this story was born.

Writing a story from the perspective of a young accountant is much different from writing from the perspective of private eye Robert Douglas. Mark, the narrator in this story, doesn't have the intuition or the detective skills to figure out the mystery. In fact, he becomes baffled at every turn. Unable to come up with a reasonable explanation of the events, he even considers wild theories of multiple personalities and parallel universes. Before we criticize the narrator too much, almost all of the readers I am aware of are just as baffled as the narrator. The very normal and logical explanation of someone impersonating his voice escapes most readers.

This story is first because it is my personal favorite. It hits the ground running with the immediate conflict of the phone call. Like the narrator, the reader (hopefully) is drawn into the story and immediately perplexed with what is going on. The tension doesn't drop as the narrator races home and the reader wonders if he will come face-to-face to the voice on the phone. Although that doesn't happen, an equally dramatic event happens, a dead body is discovered. Then, the arrest and the trial soon follows. I love writing courtroom dialogue! The story concludes with a second murder and what I believe is the most powerful ending that I have ever written.

About the Stories

This story is supported by a lot of secondary characters. Sam, Cathy, Chris, Mr. Wesley, Mrs. Wesley, and Brian all play integral parts in the plot of the story. I enjoyed writing this story so much I have racked my brain to see if there is a good plot line to write a sequel. Unfortunately, my brainstorming has come up empty. But hey, having a plot for a sequel was never a prerequisite for Hollywood!

Elevator to Nowhere

One of this story's strongest clues is right in the title. Adam and Brett got on the elevator because they thought it would take them to their therapy session. However, it turns out that their therapy session occurred in the elevator. Thus, the destination for the elevator was to nowhere.

This story leaves a little more to the reader's imagination than some of the others in this book. There's no detective or first person narrator to explain all the details of this story.

The premise of this story is simple. Dr. Downs and Dr. Van Shoran, colleagues and friends who share offices, each has a new patient, one transferred from another therapist and one court appointed. The two patients share one thing in common. Neither patient wants to attend the session, and thus likely would resist opening up about their respective feelings and emotions.

A plan was hatched. By making an early appointment before the building would normally open, Dr. Downs, posing as the security guard, let both of them in the building, as a group. The key to the plan was to get them to talk in a more relaxed environment without the perceived spotlight of being analyzed. The solution is that Dr. Van Shoran, posing as another patient named Maria, would enter an elevator with the two "real" patients. Once the elevator became stuck, Maria would steer the conversation to instill trust so the other two could reflect on their behavior. Dr. Downs, as Rusty, would monitor the conversation in the elevator. Once substantial progress was made toward reflection on their behavior and a change in their own attitudes, the elevator would be restarted.

Unfortunately, because they would be recognized, the two doctors realized they could never be continuing patients. However, once doctors had turned around the patients' perspective of therapy, the doctors knew that Adam and Brett would be more successful working with any future therapist. The doctors made only one mistake. Dr. Van Shoran accidentally left her purse behind, which turned out to spoil the secret.

This story was told from a unique perspective. The narrator acts purely as a "fly on the wall", providing no further information than what can be seen or heard. Therefore, the reader does not become privy to any background information on any of the characters unless it is seen or heard by a character in the story.

This is one of my personal favorite stories in this book because it allows me to speak out about some of my own philosophies in the context of the story. The different perspectives and arguments that the characters use are some I've used myself. However, if the reader learns nothing else from this story, I hope they realize that getting stuck in an elevator for 30 minutes wouldn't be such a bad thing. That is, if it gave them the opportunity to stop, think, and reflect on how they live their life, what causes stress in their life, and whether their actions match-up against their life priorities; then the thirty minute detainment would be a good thing.

About the Stories

Murder in a Country Town

Writing this story was just plain fun. To use an analogy, this story is like one of those wild rollercoaster rides with hairpin turns, deep drops, and a corkscrew twist at the end. And the whole ride lasts only three minutes.

The reader feels the first rollercoaster turn within the very first paragraph. The story immediately drops the reader moments before a murder. It turns out to be a red herring because it is a duck, not a person, that is on the receiving end of the gunshot.

The biggest twist of this coaster ride is when the reader realizes that Sheriff Parsons is a series character created by the author. Subtle clues included the narrator saying that he had "plotted out" Sheriff Parsons death, and would "write-off" the sheriff, who was quite a "character".

This is actually a story within a story. Did you figure out that the narrator was an author and Sheriff Parsons was a series character in his story? If so, kudos to you. But, in the narrator's story, who killed Sheriff Parsons?

Ah, not much information was given. We know there was a suicide note and two suspects: the convict and the deputy. Supposedly, the deputy rushed over to inform the sheriff that Frank had escaped during the night. The sheriff's suicide note states that he couldn't live with the fact that Frank had escaped. One question: how did Sheriff Parsons know that Frank escaped? It appears that Frank must have stopped by Sheriff Parsons' house on the way out of town.

Eric J. Lee

The Intuition of Henry Burrows

In many of my stories, I try to hit the readers with a big attention getter that jolts their interest with the hopes of immediately drawing them into the story. Not so with this story. It starts in a relaxed setting and isn't until we are one third of the way through the story that conflict (in the form of the ax murderer) appears. Like a snowball going downhill, my goal in this story is to build momentum toward a climactic conclusion.

My biggest challenge in this story was to be true to the fact that Henry's visitor was a trick-or-treater without giving it away. A big obstacle I had to contend with was how to get Henry to take candy to the front door without tipping off the reader's suspicion. My strategy was to talk about the Hershey kisses from the beginning of the story. By talking about the candy frequently, it was fair to believe that he had candy with him when he went to the front door without explicitly stating it.

I like the character of the older, but feisty Henry Burrows. I enjoyed telling a story through his eyes. Henry is a nice contrast between the sharp, but far less confident Robert Douglas, the narrator in *Someone is trying to kill me*. Who knows? Maybe the two will battle wits in a later story. Since the ax murderer didn't get him in this story, it can still happen.

For most mystery stories, you need some type of red herring to throw the reader off track. The red herring in this story is simple: the title of the story. The story was written to imply that it dealt with the intuition of an ex-inspector. Did the inspector really have the intuition to sense the impending danger? The story never even attempts to answer this. Because he was never in any danger, we never find out.

This story was read to a group of thirty adults. Granted, when you hear, as opposed to read a story, you retain less. Still, only about half figured out that the ax murderer was a trick-or-treater before the last two paragraphs. Date the story was read: October 31st.

Thus, give yourself a gold star if you figured it out and you read it at least a month away from Halloween.

The Perfect Crime

This is probably the most misunderstood story that I have ever written. Whenever someone reads this story, I usually hear them say, "Oh, the Jack and Jill nursery rhyme. You wrote an entire story about that." Now, it is true that I enjoyed having a twist at the end where the characters were Jack and Jill from the nursery rhyme. However, that was far from the point of the story.

The story was really about committing the perfect crime. In fact, I dedicated the first page of the story to outline what the perfect crime is. In the story, I say "A perfect crime occurs when the entire country knew about a crime, but no one knows who was responsible. Even better, the perfect criminal commits a crime that no one realizes was a crime." And these two sentences describe our narrator. Almost everyone in the U.S. has heard that Jack and Jill fell down the hill, but no one suspects that they were ever pushed. Even after reading the story, do you know who pushed them? The answer is no because this narrator is so perfect, he never gives his name throughout the entire story!

In continuing to look for new settings and circumstances to write about, this story is my first crime caper. It starts slowly and methodically as the characters plot out their strategy to steal the diamond. The only tension at this point is whether their heist will be successful. The story takes off at a much more tension-filled pace when Johnny finds the diamond is no longer embedded in the well.

Now, for the Jack and Jill gimmick, I initially felt that I gave too many clues. A male and a female, one who is "called Johnny" and other named Jill. And then I bring into the story a pail, a hill, and the water well. However, most readers are surprised when the gimmick is revealed.

Pay Up

At only 700 words, Pay Up is the shortest story in this book (not counting the poem *The Death of Seth*). I enjoy writing stories of this length. However, it does pose a challenge to develop vivid characters, a strong climax, and a satisfying conclusion in a very short amount of time. It forces me to be disciplined, writing economically to make each word count.

I like the opening of Pay Up. I wanted to make an emotional impact in the first two words of the story (which mirror the title) by immediately showing conflict. Then, by using the words, "table" and "meager cash left", I tried to paint the picture of a high-stakes poker game. Using the description of Big Vinny with a crooked smile and a cigar wedged in his mouth was an effort to further this picture.

The middle part of this story is a flashback. Usually, I'm not a fan of flashbacks, finding them either anti-climactic or confusing for the reader. For this flashback and thus the story to be effective, my opening had to be convincing as some type of high-stakes poker game.

Once I decided to write a story about Monopoly, I studied the board to decide how to incorporate the game into the story. I anguished over the decision to use street names from the Monopoly game, but in the end, decided that was too much of a hint. So, the description of the first property near the railroad tracks being on Vermont Avenue became a rewrite casualty.

I won't recount all of the other clues hinting this was a Monopoly game. You can reread the story and find them. If you look hard, you'll find even innocuous phrases such as being "on a roll" and "every chance I took" point toward the game of Monopoly.

Once when I visited my uncle, I asked him if he had a Monopoly set.

"Sure, would you like me to get it?" he asked.

"Yes, please," I responded.

"So, you want to play?" he surmised, looking forward to playing.

"No," I said, shaking my head. A puzzled look crossed his face. "It's research," I explained. The puzzled look on my uncle's face remained. Finally, he shrugged his shoulders and handed me the board, probably thinking I was crazy.

That's okay. All good mystery writers are crazy, right?

Someone is Trying to Kill Me

Robert Douglas, the private eye, is back as the narrator. This is my second story featuring Robert, who narrated *Disappearing Act*, a story I wrote years earlier. With the brown hat and working man attitude, I wanted to conjure up the image of the classic private eye.

Writing a sequel to an earlier story is challenging and fun. It's like a class reunion. In writing this story, I was returning to the character of Robert Douglas and the "small town" setting around him. The truth is I had to reread *Disappearing Act* several times so I could stay true to Robert's character and relationship with the local police department. Robert is clever and a quick thinker, but he's not a "know it all." He struggles along with the reader to piece clues together. His biggest attribute is that he's resourceful and is not afraid to seek the aid of others. Officer Petersen, the only recurring character besides Robert from *Disappearing Act*, has now been promoted to senior deputy and becomes a great ally to Robert in getting to the truth.

This story is really divided into two parts. In the first part, the reader and narrator are left to wonder whether Margaret was in any real danger. And if she was, from whom? This tension and uncertainty keeps the reader's interest until we have the murder half way through the story. The second half of the story follows Robert as he works to solve the mystery.

This is my first story that I ever wrote in which inheritance was a motive for murder. A slight pet peeve, I think "murder for money" is overdone as a motive for killing a family member. So, I enjoyed using that as the red herring for a murder motive. Further complicating the issue is the fact that the reader is tricked into thinking that Margaret was the victim. There are clues that would lead you to doubt this, such as the fact that there were no distinguishable remains of the body and, at the same time, Cathy's mysterious disappearance. Also, Robert, a self-proclaimed good judge of character, stated that Margaret appeared to be "acting" fearful.

Death of Seth

Each of my books includes one story in the format of a rhyming poem. Before becoming a mystery author, I wrote poetry. Often, I miss writing poetry. Usually, that feeling disappears once I try to write a poem. For me, poetry takes discipline and an unbelievable amount of patience. I can literally spend thirty minutes trying to write two lines of a poem.

But, once I've completed a poem, I have a feeling of satisfaction that's unmatched from a story. But, with hours of work and only a few words to show for it, I am always left with a "never again" feeling.

It's my guess that very few people figured out that the narrator is the woman. She's just looking at herself in the mirror. Despite this, there are very real clues in this extremely short story.

First, I disclosed that the woman was in a bathroom. Almost every bathroom in the world has a mirror. Second, the narrator's actions repeatedly "mirror" the movements of the woman. The story states, "I started to cry" and "tears rolled down her bruised face", "I winked at the woman and she winked back", and "I took a deep breath and the woman did the same".

But, this story was more than a wise guy mystery writer looking to throw a twist at the reader. This story has nothing to do with split personalities. It's simply how the narrator looks into the mirror and can no longer identify with the picture. The narrator does not see herself as a scared, frightened, trembling person. So anytime the story refers to a scared, beaten person, the narrator looks in the mirror and says "her" or "the woman". However, "I" is used when the narrator is trying to resolve or deal with the problem.

When the Personals Get Personal

I was once asked, "Do you ever get tired of writing mystery stories?" I thought about it for only two seconds before responding, "No". I believe I avoid ever getting "tired" or "bored" by writing different characters, different perspectives, and different levels of suspense.

This story starts with a personal ad, which actually includes one of the strongest clues of the story. The clue is the following sentence, "We shared a joke together about another passenger." I had some strong misgivings about such a big clue at the very beginning of the story. I never mind when a reader figures out a solution to the story. In fact, I'd like about 15-20% of the readers to do so before they finish reading the story. However, I never want the reader to figure it out from the very beginning. However, from my research, this clue seems to go unnoticed and most readers don't figure out that Karen is being tricked until the very end.

This story is told in the third person with the clear main character being a young woman named Karen. I usually take a liking to all of the main characters in my stories, but not so with Karen. She's self absorbed and sees people very superficially. Several people have asked me why I didn't name the "pudgy man". I did this intentionally. Since the story was told from Karen's perspective, the man's name was irrelevant. To her, he was just a pudgy man with whom she had to talk.

I received some grief from some readers for describing the character as the "pudgy man" rather than naming him. I wanted to drill into the reader's mind (since it was already fully consuming Karen's mind) the fact that he was overweight. You will note once he leaves the table at the end of the story, he is only referred to as a "man" with the word "pudgy" dropped.

I write both murder mystery and suspense stories. As a result, I like that the reader never knows whether one of my stories will include a murder or not. In this story, Allison's paranoia about the meeting and insistence that Karen bring mace alert the reader to a possible upcoming danger. Little did Karen know that the damage that would hit her would not be physical, but psychological and economic.

About the Stories

The Confession

This story is unique in that it is not a "Who done it?", but a "Who will do it?" The story is told from Father John Flockhart's perspective. I wrote him as a likable character that has been pushed into a world a chaos and poor decisions.

The story begins with the suspense of Sam's confession of the large theft. Then, the stakes get raised with Carl's confession of the hit. This transforms Sam from initial bad guy to unfortunate victim.

I wanted to keep a high level of suspense throughout the story. Some readers may have felt the ending was abrupt. Once that Ellen was revealed to be a temporary employee, I felt that the unmasking of the hitman (or hitwoman in this case) had to happen soon. And with no one wanting the police involved, there was little that needed to be said after her reveal.

There were not many overt clues that Ellen was the hitperson. However, if Charlie made arrangements for the hitman before he died, then we know the hitman would be in that building around 5:00. With Steven eliminated as a suspect as a long time friend of Sam's, that leaves only Father John, Carl, and Ellen. It simply did not make sense that either John or Carl would be the hired killer. Thus, the reader could likely deduce Ellen was the culprit.

Other short story collections by this author:

This book features nine short mystery and suspense stories. In the short story, *Murder in a Coastal Town*, a homicide detective, is overcome with grief at the murder of his eight-year-old son. The only witness to the murder is his eleven-year-old daughter. How does he extract detailed information about the murder from a witness who is desperately trying to forget? Will the detective ever be able to catch the murderer and what emotional price is he willing to pay?

In another story, the reader is dropped in the jury box of a high profile murder case. The senator's husband could be facing the death penalty. Private eye and jury member Robert Douglas is used to solving cases, but how will he be able to convince eleven strangers to adopt his perspective on the case.

For more information about the author and his stories, please visit his official website at www.ericleestories.com

Other short story collections by this author:

This book features nine short mystery and suspense stories. In the short story, *Murder in a Coastal Town*, a homicide detective, is overcome with grief at the murder of his eight-year-old son. The only witness to the murder is his eleven-year-old daughter. How does he extract detailed information about the murder from a witness who is desperately trying to forget? Will the detective ever be able to catch the murderer and what emotional price is he willing to pay?

In another story, four guests arrive separately to a gated mansion. They realize they all played a central role in the conviction of Carols Rivera ten years earlier. They soon meet their host for the evening: recent prison escapee, Carols Rivera.

For more information about the author and his stories, please visit his official website at www.ericleestories.com

Other novels by this author:

Trying to Win at Love tells the funny and inspiring story of a new tennis captain pressed into running a local team because "there's no one else." As his own expectations for success rise, the rookie captain begins to equate wins as validation from his players and competitors. His troubles, which aren't limited to the court, soon mount as quickly as his victories. A group of colorful characters and extraordinary events teach him valuable lessons about winning on the court and in life.

For more information about the author and his stories, please visit his official website at www.ericleestories.com.

Other novels by this author:

In this humorous and inspiring sequel to the novel *Trying to Win at Love*, the narrator copes with several stinging losses. Faced with new challenges, he discovers that old approaches don't always provide the solution. Without the comfort and familiarity of the past, he struggles in his attempt to find a new team and mend a broken heart. In the process, he learns a lot about himself and life as he once again tries to win at love.

For more information about the author and his stories, please visit his official website at www.ericleestories.com.